Gypsy

Gypsy

Dan Foley

A
Grinning Skull Press
Publication

ISBN: 0-9986912-0-8 (paperback)
ISBN-13: 978-0-9986912-0-6 (paperback)
ISBN: 978-0-9986912-1-3 (e-book)

DEDICATION

For my sister, Joy.

CONTENTS

Chapter One

Barkham, Vermont, July, 1956

Stu Miller strutted around the Barkham fair as if he owned it. He was definitely the Alpha-dog to the group of five men who trailed along at his heels. At six-foot-seven and two hundred and fifty pounds, Miller was a giant of a man, and not a gentle giant at that. He was a loud-talking, misogynistic bully who took pride in terrorizing the residents of Barkham and the surrounding area.

Fairgoers moved to the side and conversations stopped when Miller and his cronies passed. They didn't ride any rides, they didn't play any games of chance. They just swaggered through the crowds, basking in their notoriety. The one time Miller stopped, it was for the ring-the-bell challenge. It was fifty cents for three tries.

"Somebody give me half a buck," he told his crew.

Bill Burke and Bucky St. John each dug a quarter out of their pockets and handed them over. Miller gave them to the attendant and got the heavy mallet designed to hinder, not help, whoever was swinging it. He hefted it and laughed for the crowd of onlookers that had gathered to see the big man swing it. Most, if not all of them, were hoping he would fail.

Stu brought the mallet down with the practiced swing he used when splitting logs for customers. It struck the padded end of the fulcrum and sent the weight on the pole rushing upward. A second later the bell at the top of the pole rang with a loud *clang*. Two more swings were followed by two more *clangs*.

"Anybody else? How about one of you guys?" He stepped back and held the mallet out to his boys. Even though two of them, Bill Burke and Sawyer Gaunt, could have rung the bell, neither of them stepped up. After years of hanging with Stu, they both knew better than to accept the challenge. Baker, who was the runt of the group, wouldn't have had a chance. He had stopped growing in high school and only stood at five-foot-four and weighed in at a hundred and thirty pounds.

When no one took him up on his offer, Stu flexed his biceps for the crowd, dropped the mallet, and strutted off, basking in his glory as the crowd parted before him. Looks of disapproval and outright hate followed him.

He stopped when he saw the gypsy and her sign at the end of the midway. Gold letters on a red background proclaimed: *Palms Read, Fortunes Told, $1.*

The gypsy was hot ... hot, hot, hot, and Big Stu Miller knew hot. And he knew that *she* knew that she looked hot standing outside the tent in her gypsy costume: a scarf covering most of her jet black hair, big hoop earrings, peasant blouse that couldn't hide impressive tits, and a billowing skirt that went all the way to the ground. He had a feeling the rest of her was as impressive as the tits. *Aw, what the hell! It was only a buck.*

"Wait here," he told the men with him. "I'm going to check this broad out."

There was no question that they would. Back in high school, they had called themselves the "Fearsome Five," or "Stu's Crew." He thought of them as the "Fearful Five." Without him, they were just a bunch of pussies.

When Stu handed over the dollar, the woman led him into the darkened tent. Together, they could have been part of the midway oddities. Miller towered over the woman, who was barely five-two. Inside, it smelled of incense, and the air was at least ten degrees cooler than it had been outside. There was a table in the middle of the room with a black cloth draped over it that reached to the ground. A crystal ball sat atop the table in the center of a pentagram. Arcane symbols were scattered at random points around it.

When the gypsy sat down, she motioned for Stu to take the chair opposite her. "Would you prefer tarot cards or the crystal ball?"

"Cards, I guess." Stu didn't care what she used. In his mind he was already undressing her, caressing those magnificent tits, forcing himself into her.

Without a word, the gypsy removed the ball from the table. Then she placed a deck of cards in front of him, face down. She fanned them out in one quick, practiced motion. "Choose five."

She took them from him one at a time and in the order he had selected them. She then placed them on the table, one at each point of the pentagram. When she was done, she reached out and turned over the first card he had selected. "This is your card. The Fool. It —"

Big Stu's anger flared. "Are you calling me a fool? Nobody calls me a fool!" Actually, pretty much everyone except his crew called him a fool, just not to his face. Not since he had broken Alan Granito's arm for it anyway.

"No, The Fool represents —"

Stu didn't wait to hear any more. "Don't call me a fool!" he yelled as he jumped up, overturning the table and scattering the cards everywhere.

"I —"

Before she could say anything else, Stu stormed from the tent with his fists balled, fury turning his face red. The bitch would pay.

The men who had waited for him — Hubie Martin, Sawyer Gaunt, Bill Burke, Bucky St. John, and Jack Baker — knew something had pissed him off. "Oh, shit," St. John mumbled low enough so Miller wouldn't hear.

"Let's go! We're out of here," Stu growled when he reached them. Not one of the men said a word; they just followed along behind him in silence. Each of them knew Stu well enough to know he was going to take his anger out on someone and they didn't want it to be them.

"Meet me at my place," Miller said before storming off to the parking lot.

* * *

Stu was sitting outside, working on his second cold one when his crew arrived. St. John and Baker and were in Baker's Hudson. Gaunt, Martin, and Burke were in Gaunt's Chevy Belair. "Grab a beer and gather around," he told them when they reached him. Each of the men snagged one from the cooler and then sat on the logs Miller used as makeshift chairs.

"That bitch gypsy called me a fool. Nobody calls me a fool. Meet me here at midnight and we'll go over and pay her a little visit."

Each of the men felt relief because they weren't the target of his anger. Excitement coursed through them because they knew what he had in mind. They'd done it before.

* * *

Even though the gypsy's trailer was set apart from rest of the carnival's caravan, it was still close enough that any noise they made could draw an angry crowd of carnies. "Quiet," Stu hissed. The warning was unneeded since each man knew what would happen if they were caught sneaking around the gypsy's trailer. Big Stu wanted the bitch; the extra men were just there for insurance. They all knew they'd get their turn when Stu was finished with her.

The lock on the trailer's door was flimsy enough that Stu was able to snap it open when he applied his weight to it.

Inside, the trailer was dimly illuminated by light streaming in from the fairground. The bitch was sleeping on a double bed at the opposite end. He had no more problem slapping a hand over her mouth and carrying her out of the trailer than a normal-sized man would have had with a small child. Once outside, Stu carted her off to the nearby woods with his crew of cronies jockeying for position behind him.

When he was in the woods, Stu threw the gypsy on the ground and ripped off her night clothes. She proved to be as fine as he had thought she would be. "Who's the fool now, bitch?" he sneered as he forced himself into her. The whole thing only lasted a few minutes. Then Stu left her to the rest of his crew.

There was a definite pecking order among the five. St. John was first, followed by Burke, Martin, Gaunt, and, finally, Baker. Because he was the smallest and always went last at anything they did, Baker was also the meanest. He took Celeste from behind, grabbing her hair and pulling her head back so far her neck almost snapped. All the while he was thrusting into her, he cursed her for a whore and slapped her ass with his free hand.

When they were done, they left her in the woods, lying naked, battered, bruised, and abused. The carnies found her the next morning after finding the door to the trailer open and the lock broken.

Chapter Two

Barkham, Vermont, July, 2006

Tim was daydreaming and almost rear ended the last car in a long line of vehicles that were barely creeping along the road in front of him. *What the hell? Must be an accident. Maybe I should flip a U-e? If it completely stops, I will. If not, I guess I'll stick it out.*

Ten minutes later the cause of the slowdown became apparent. It was the annual Barkham summer fair. *What the hell, I can't remember the last time I've been to a fair. I won't get another chance, so I might as well go in. Besides, I think I hear a nice, greasy pepper, onion, and sausage grinder calling me.*

After paying ten dollars for parking and another ten for entrance to the fair itself, Tim went in search of the grinder that had already cost him twenty bucks. By the time he finally took his first bite, he could add another seven for the grinder and two for the Coke to go with it.

What the hell, it's only money, right? he thought as he strolled between brightly lit rides and fair booths.

Was it worth it? Definitely. The grinder was actually as good as he remembered. The fat would play hell with his bowels after so many years of "healthy" eating, but hey, healthy had gone out the door when old man cancer had walked in.

Licking the grease from his fingers (*Damn, it was good!*), he sucked down the last of the Coke and looked for somewhere to toss the empty. No trash cans were handy, so he dropped it between two of the games of chance that had replaced the rides. Then he aimlessly made his way through the crowd, knowing there wouldn't be too many more days like this one.

A gaggle of teenaged girls blew by him, followed by a group of boys obviously trying to keep up. *Oh, to be that young again.* He nodded at a biker and his tattooed girlfriend and the biker nodded back. Nothing he'd do in front of a bar, but this was a fair — everybody was cool at a fair. He thought about going on a few rides, maybe the Ferris wheel. He actually bought a book of tickets. When his stomach growled, he remembered the grease-filled grinder and Coke. *With my luck, I'll get to the top of the wheel and either puke or need to use the bathroom.* The tickets went to a pair of kids who thanked him and ran off toward the Tilt-A-Whirl. More power to them.

Eventually, his wandering brought him back around to the games of chance.

Get three softballs in the basket — win a prize; knock over the milk bottles — win a prize; toss your quarter onto the red circle — win a prize. Christ, these things haven't changed since I was a kid.

8

He reached the end of the row and was about to turn around and head back up the opposite side when he noticed a solitary booth sitting at the edge of the fairgrounds. There was a sign outside that looked like it had seen better days. Gold letters on a red background proclaimed: *Palms Read, Fortunes Told, $10.*

An old woman dressed as a gypsy sat just inside. She looked up from the cards she was placing on the table in front of her and beckoned him to come over with nothing more than a knowing tilt of her head. When he met her eyes, he felt drawn to her. He almost ignored her, almost turned around, but in the end, he walked into her tent.

"Do you want to know your future?"

Tim gave her a wry smile. "I already know my future."

A shiver ran up his spine when she said, "You think you do. But you don't. Sit down and I'll tell you."

Tim shook the feeling off, attributing it the temperature change from the outside to the inside of the tent. Then he thought, *Why not. At least it'll be good for a laugh.* He took a ten from his wallet and placed it on the table in front of her. He expected the bill to disappear as if it had never been there, but she never touched it.

"Give me your hand."

He did, and flinched when a spark seemed to pass between them. The woman must have felt it, too, because her eyes widened in surprise. She held it, palm open, and traced a finger along what he assumed was his life line. The spark he had felt when they had first touched followed the tip of her finger as it moved along his palm. The hairs on the back of his neck stood up when she closed his hand and held it in both of hers. *How does she do that?* he wondered.

"You've received some very bad news. The cancer that is eating your body is almost done. You have three … four months at the most. Soon the pain will come. You will need medicine to live with it. I'm sorry."

Tim was stunned. The doctors had told him the very same thing the day before.

"How did … ?" he started to ask, but she cut him off.

"It doesn't have to be this way. I can show you a different path."

"What do you mean a different path? Cancer is cancer. It's gone too far. No one can help me."

"I can."

Ah, here it comes. She's put the bait out there, now she wants to see if I'll bite.

"I don't blame you for being skeptical. I would be, too, if I were you. But if you want to live, hear me out."

What the hell? I've gone this far, I might as well see what she has to say. "And how do you intend to do that?"

"Come back tomorrow at noon and I'll show you."

Tim shook his head. "I don't think so."

"Well, it's your choice. My offer is good until noon tomorrow."

When Tim turned to leave, she gave him back his ten dollars along with a tarot card … The Fool.

Puzzled, Tim took the bill and the card. "Why are you giving my money back, and what's the card for?"

"Return tomorrow and I'll tell you everything. Make sure you bring the card with you."

Crazy, Tim thought, but he took the money and

the card. He spent another hour wandering around the fair before deciding he'd had enough. He might have stayed longer, but a few stomach cramps were enough to convince him he should head home.

"You coming back?" the man at the gate asked as Tim was leaving.

"Maybe. Why?"

"Better let me stamp your hand then. Your admission fee is good for two days if you show your stamp."

"Why can't I just show you my admission ticket?"

"It prevents people from giving their ticket away. They can't give their stamp away, can they?"

"I guess not," Tim admitted. "What about parking?"

"Parking's free as long as you have your ticket and you show them your stamp."

* * *

Celeste Conti was shaking when the man she had waited fifty years for walked out of her tent. She didn't know if he would return. If he did, she would never know it. Not in this lifetime anyway.

Chapter Three

Wayne, New Jersey, September 3rd, 1964

Kristin Ritter left the library later than she had planned. She had gotten so wrapped up in the paper she was working on that she completely lost track of the time. When she stepped outside, it was already full dark. She could go back inside and ask someone to accompany her to her car, but she was already late.

The ten-minute walk was mostly well lit, but there was one section where the light on a pole was out. Half way through it, a hand clamped over her mouth and an arm grabbed her around the waist. "Scream and you're dead," a rough male voice whispered in her ear.

Her attacker dragged her into a nearby copse of rhododendrons, ripped her panties off, and raped her from behind. She never saw his face. The only thing she could tell the police was that he was big and white.

Even though the rape wasn't her fault, it ruined

her life. As bad as the rape had been, it was the feelings of guilt and shame that changed her from an outgoing girl who loved life to a withdrawn, fearful soul. Everyone at school seemed to be staring at her, but they quickly glanced away when she looked at them. Conversations stopped when she walked into a room. Her boyfriend broke up with her. Her father avoided her, and her mother seemed to ooze pity. The only one who didn't treat her like an outcast was her brother. But Tim was in Vietnam and they could only talk by phone.

"I never should have reported it. I should have just kept my mouth shut," she told him over the static of a tenuous connection. She wished he could put his arm around her shoulders and hug her, but he couldn't. All he could do was listen to her and tell her he loved her.

The next morning, her father found her hanging from a rafter in the one-car garage behind the house.

Tim was in the bush and didn't hear about it until two weeks later.

Chapter Four

Barkham, Vermont, July, 2006

The gypsy's promise plagued Tim, keeping sleep at bay. He was seventy-two. If it wasn't for the cancer spreading throughout his body, he could have had another ten or twenty good years ahead of him instead of the three to four pain-filled months the doctors said he had. *I should go back. It won't cost anything. I'm going to do it*, he thought before finally falling asleep.

In the morning, Tim lay in bed staring at the ceiling. *What was I thinking? It was all just some sort of scam. I'd be a fool to go back.* When he got out of bed, the wave of nausea that came with standing up, and the thought of a future filled with hospitals and pain killers, changed his mind. He knew he was grasping at straws, but like a drowning man, he would reach out for anything that offered even a glimmer of hope.

* * *

When he pulled up to the fair entrance and showed his parking pass to the attendant, the man asked, "You got your stamp?"

Tim held his left hand out the window. "Right here."

The man smiled and waved him on. "Good enough. Have fun at the fair, and don't forget to spend your money."

Spend my money. That's why they let people back in. They want us to come back and spend our money. Somebody was thinking when they came up with that.

"Don't worry, I intend to," he told the guy who mouthed the same greeting about spending his money when he showed his stamp at the fair's entry point.

Tim retraced the route he had taken the previous day to the fortune teller's tent. At first, everything was the same. The unmistakable aroma of pepper, onion, and sausage grinders called to him. He was tempted to stop for another one until he looked at his watch. *Maybe later, after I meet the gypsy.* The fried dough booth he passed by almost made him delay his trip to the woman's tent, but he resisted.

When he turned the corner onto the section of the midway with the games of chance, his vision blurred and he experienced a moment of vertigo. He attributed it to the tumor growing in his brain.

What is this? A Dress-Like-the-Fifties Day? Tim thought as he made his way through the crowd. Shorts and tee-shirts had been replaced by long pants and short-sleeved shirts on the men. Dresses had replaced shorts and tank tops on the women. Boys in cuffed jeans ran from booth to booth looking for the best chance of winning a prize. He could see the gypsy's tent at the end of the midway, but it looked newer than it had yesterday. Then a barker's call stopped him in his tracks. "Three balls for a quarter, folks. Three balls for a quarter. Knock the bottles down and win a prize."

A quarter? These games haven't cost a quarter since I was a kid. Then he got it. It was all part of the Dress-Like-the-Fifties Day. Even the sign outside the gypsy's tent had been changed. It was still red with gold letters, but this time it read: *Palms Read, Fortunes Told, $1.*

His first thought was, *I could have saved myself nine bucks.* His second was, *I bet she gets a lot more business for a buck than she did for ten.*

Tim's next surprise came when he entered the tent and found a young woman sitting behind the table. "Where's the old woman who was here yesterday?" he asked when he saw her.

The young woman gave him a puzzled look before answering. "What old woman? I was here yesterday."

Is this part of the scam? A bait and switch? Tim took the tarot card from his pocket and held it out. "The old woman who gave me this told me to come back today at noon."

The gypsy took the card and, after turning it over in her hands and examining it, asked him, "When are you from?"

"St. Johnsbury."

"Not where. When. *When* are you from? What year do you think this is?"

"What year do I think this is? I know what year it is. It's 2006."

The woman, girl really, looked at him with hungry eyes. It had been a long time since any woman had looked at him like that, let alone someone as young and pretty as this one. Then she shocked him by saying, "No, it's 1956. Now sit down and tell me everything I told you yesterday."

"*You* didn't tell me anything," he insisted. "I talked to an old woman yesterday. I don't know what you people are up to, but I've had enough. I'm leaving."

Before he could go, she reached out and touched his cheek. He felt the same spark he had felt when the old woman had touched his hand the day before. "Come back when you realize where you are, and when you are. I'll be here. Just don't take too long. We're leaving tomorrow.

Right, come back when I realize when I am. Like that's going to happen.

Tim retraced his footsteps past the turn in the midway where he had first encountered the 50s style attire. This time the entire fair and all the people in it were dressed as though they were from the 1950s. The fried dough stand had been replaced by a cotton candy stall. The grinder trailer was now a hamburger and hot dog stand. *What the hell is this? It's all changed. They can't all be in on this scam, can they?*

All doubts that it was an elaborate prank evaporated when he reached the exit to the parking lot. The newest cars he could see were a 1955 Ford and a 1955 Chevy. The Ford was sitting next to a bullet nose Studebaker. There were cars and pickups from the forties all the way up to the Ford and Chevy. Not one was newer than that.

Oh shit! This is real, he told himself, then staggered back to the gypsy's tent.

"You're back. You believe me now?"

"What's happening? How did you do this?"

"Tell me everything that I told you yesterday. Then I can tell you what happened."

"I came to you. You read my palm. You knew I had cancer. You knew I only had months to live. You told me that if I helped you, you could help me. You gave me that tarot card and told me to come back to-day."

"Give me your hands," she told Tim. He did — and felt the spark pass between them when they touched.

"If you had cancer then, you don't have it now."

"That's impossible. Cancer just doesn't go away."

"It didn't go away. You left it behind."

"What do you mean I 'left it behind'? I've seen the X-rays. I've seen the test results."

"Have you seen *this*?" she asked, and handed him a mirror.

Tim peered into it, but the image was blurry. He shook his head, took off his glasses, and the image sharpened into a much younger version of himself. A version before the cancer had started growing inside him. As he watched, the face in the mirror continued to shed the years that had aged it.

* * *

Celeste had felt the spark that passed between them when they touched. She knew what had happened even if he didn't. For her, the rape had only happened two days ago. For him, her rape was fifty years in the past. He had met her in his lifetime after a life she hadn't lived yet. When he turned and walked from her tent, her heart sank. Could she really have waited fifty years for him only to have him turn and walk away?

Would she have to wait another fifty years, or longer, to find the man she needed?

Chapter Five

Barkham, Vermont, 1956

Stu didn't look up when he heard the car pull to a stop. He knew who it was, and why he was there, but he didn't care. "Morning, Sheriff. Something I can do for you?" he asked, still not looking up when his brother's polished shoes and blue uniform pants walked into his vision.

"I got a complaint about you today. Girl from the carnival says you and a bunch of other men raped her."

"That so?"

"Yep."

"And?"

"And I took care of it. But this has got to stop. You're going to pick on the wrong person one of these days, and I'm not going to be able smooth it over."

Stu finally looked up from the chainsaw he was

working on. "Why don't you let me worry about that? Nobody around here is ever going to be a problem. You know that as well as I do."

"Yeah, well I'm just saying. Tone it down a notch, will you?"

"Sure, anything for you."

"Yeah, right. Just cool it. If this had been a local girl instead of one of those carnies, it could have been a real problem."

"Well, it wasn't, so don't get your panties in a knot. I don't shit where I eat. I'm not stupid, you know."

And there was the problem. He was that stupid ... or just that arrogant.

Chapter Six

When Tim's reflection finally stopped growing younger, the face staring back at him was the twenty-two-year-old one he had worn in 1956. He put the mirror down and examined the rest of his body. The fingers that had been starting to curl with arthritis were straight, unmarred by knots and bumps. The faded U.S. Army Ranger tattoo that had adorned his right forearm since 1965 was gone. It had been replaced by clear, un-blemished skin. Lifting his shirt to examine his stomach, he found that even the shrapnel scars had disappeared. Looking at the unmarked skin, he realized that the metal fragments that had torn into his body and nearly taken his life were still eleven years in the future.

He was so astonished he almost didn't hear the woman when she spoke. "Look at me. Look close. What do you see?"

She was a beauty. Long black hair fell past her shoulders. Hoop earrings dangled from her ears. Bright red lipstick accented full lips, but he could see the bruises underneath the makeup. She pulled down the front of the peasant blouse to the top of her breasts, where the bruises got worse. She stood up and lifted her skirt. Her thighs were a mass of contusions and mottled skin. "Two days ago I was dragged from my trailer and raped by six men. When I went to the police, the sheriff all but laughed at me. He wanted to know what I did to encourage them. He wanted to know how much I charged."

The words struck Tim like a blow. Images of Kristen flooded his mind. "What has that got to do with me? Why are you telling me this?"

"If you came here from 2006, it means it took me fifty years to find you. Fifty years to find the man who would avenge me."

"Avenge you? What do you mean avenge you?"

"Exactly what I said. You are the justice I have waited for. The man I have saved myself for. You are my Avenger, my Destiny. And I am yours. Avenge me, stay with me, and live a different, cancer-free life. The life you were supposed to live."

"How am I supposed to avenge you?"

"I don't know. I only know that you're the one. Do you know what the card I gave you means?"

Tim took it back from her and looked at it — The Fool, a jester about to walk off a cliff. He carried a staff with a sack tied to it over his shoulder. A white dog was running beside him at his feet. "No."

"It means you are embarking on a journey, a new life. A life unlike the one you've known. You're going to become a new you."

Tim thought about what she said. For some reason he couldn't explain, it appealed to him. Maybe it was the chance at a new life. Maybe it was the woman her-self. Maybe she *was* his destiny, the part of his life that he had always thought was missing. Every time he touched her, he felt it. *This is crazy. I don't even know this woman's name and I'm going to agree to this? I should just walk away. But I can't. I don't know why, but I can't.* Then he thought of Kristen. Maybe this was a chance to avenge her, too.

"If I agree to this, when do we start?"

"Now," she answered, and spread a deck of cards face down on the table in front of him. She reached out, slid one from the deck, and placed it in front of her, next to The Fool. "Now you pick one."

Tim reached over and slid one from the pile. The gypsy took it and placed it in the center of the penta-gram drawn on the cloth covering the table.

"Now draw five more."

As he did, she took them and placed one at each point of the pentagram.

When she was done, she turned over the one she had chosen and placed next to his — The Lovers. The card needed no explanation.

Then she turned over the first card he had chosen, the one she had placed at the center of the pentagram. It was The Emperor. "This is the leader, the man they all follow. This is the one who carried me from my trailer. He was the first to rape me while the others stood and watched. Then he gave me to them."

Tim started to ask who the man was, and then realized he didn't know who *she* was. "If I'm going do this, I should at least know your name."

"Later. First this," she told him as she turned over each of the cards he had chosen.

They were The Moon, Judgement, Death, The

Devil, and The Chariot.

"What do they mean?"

"Only you can say what they mean. Study them, let them talk to you. One card for each of the men that circle the Emperor. When each man's time comes, the cards will tell you what they want."

Tim was confused, but he didn't argue. Then she answered his other question. "My name is Celeste Conti. I was born in northern Italy in 1936. My parents sent me to this country in 1939 to escape the Germans in Europe. My kind was not welcome there."

"Your kind?"

"Gypsies."

"Your parents sent you? They didn't come with you?"

"No, they couldn't leave. They sent me with a family who wanted a child but couldn't have one."

"Were they gypsies, too?"

"In the old country, yes, but not here. Here, my new father found a job in a factory. He hated it, but it was all he could find. He joined the army in 1941 when the United States entered the war. He died in Normandy. My new mother was killed in an accident in 1952. The carnival was in town. I was sixteen and pretty. They took me in. I was a gypsy; carnival life came easy to me. I've been here ever since. Now, you tell me about yourself."

"My Name is Tim ... Timothy ... Ritter. I was born in 1934. I ..." Tim's voice trailed off when he realized most of what he was going to tell her hadn't happened to him yet. Most, or all of it, never would in this new life. He was twenty-two and sitting in a fortune teller's tent in Vermont. He had never even seen Vermont until he moved there in 1970.

Celeste must have sensed his dilemma. "That's all right. Tell me about the man you were."

The man I was. The seventy-two-year-old man in a twenty-two-year-old body.

"If this is July of 1956, I should still be in New Jersey. My ..." He started to tell her about Kristen, but didn't. Some things still hurt too much to talk about. "I'll join the army in 1960. After boot camp, I'll be sent to Vietnam." Vietnam was something else he didn't want to talk about. Vietnam had changed him from a naïve boy to a callous warrior. It had taken him years to put that behind him.

"I don't want to talk about my old life. It's over." *But is it? If I went to Jersey now, could I meet myself? How is this possibly happening?*

"I understand," Celeste told him.

Do you? I doubt it. I have all these memories of things that will never happen, friendships I will never make, women I will never love. How can you understand that? You can't. You never will.

Tim looked at his watch and realized it was nearing four o'clock and he hadn't eaten yet. Before he could say, "I'm hungry," Celeste reached across the table and took his wrist. Once again he felt the spark that seemed to jump between them every time they touched. "What's this?"

"My watch."

"Where are the hands? Why are there only numbers?"

"Because it's digital," he answered, and then realized that the digital watch hadn't been around in 1956. This time shift was going to take some getting used to.

Celeste seemed to be amazed by it. "I've never seen one like that. Where did you get it?"

He started to tell her "Walmart," but there weren't any Walmarts here, were there? He couldn't remember any being around back then — now. He had to stop this.

"They haven't been invented yet. I'd better get rid of it."

Celeste held out her hand. "Can I see it first?"

"Sure," Tim replied, and slipped it off his wrist.

"I'm hungry," he told her as she marveled at the watch. "How about we get something to eat? I'll buy."

"How?" Celeste asked.

"How? I've got over a hundred dollars in my wallet. That should be a small fortune now." Then he realized the problem. His money was no good here. It wouldn't be good for another fifty years or so.

Celeste saw the look of dismay on his face and knew what had just occurred to him. "Maybe I better buy."

"Maybe you better," he agreed.

"Aren't you worried about your tent?" Tim asked as they walked toward the concession stands. All she had done when they left was pull some curtains across the entrance and hang a CLOSED sign outside.

"No one will bother it. If they try, the people who work the carnival will deal with them."

For Tim, dinner consisted of two cheeseburgers, a plate of fries, and a Coke in a glass bottle. Celeste refused to eat anything from the midway. Instead, she took him back to her trailer, where she made herself a tuna fish salad.

Seeing her trailer made him realize another thing that hadn't occurred to him until now. "I don't have anywhere to stay tonight. I sure can't go home. The house I live in hasn't been built yet. I don't even have a car to sleep in."

"You can stay here with me."

Tim looked, but didn't see a bed. Ah, there it was, in the back. A couch that ran the width of the trailer. It took him a minute to realize it would unfold into a full-size double bed. "Where? There's only one bed?"

"So?"

"You mean sleep together? Are you sure?"

"Yes, but that's all we'll do. Sleep."

Tim was having a hard time asking her the big question, but he finally managed to get it out. "Who are the people who raped you?"

"I only know the one. The Emperor."

"Why do you call him The Emperor? What's his name?"

"I don't know his name. I call him The Emperor because that's the card you drew for him. He was the leader of the group of men who ..."

"How am I going to find him if I don't know his name?"

"That'll be easy. He's a giant of a man, at least six-foot-six, or six-foot-seven. He has red hair and a beard."

Oh great, Paul "Fucking" Bunyan. She wants me to whack Paul Bunyan.

"What do you want me to do to this guy?"

"I want him to die. Before he dies, I want you to make him suffer like I suffered. He took my virginity, my dignity, my life. I can never get that back."

"I can do that," he told her, and thought back to his days in Nam. He had done a lot in Nam he'd tried to forget. He thought about the first time he had killed a man. It had sickened him, but over time and count-less deaths, he had become indifferent to it. He'd had to in order to keep his sanity. He would have to bring that man back.

"I want you to make them all pay for what they did, especially the little one. He's a sadist. He enjoyed hurting me."

Chapter Seven

Tim looked around the trailer. Except for the tiny bathroom, it was just a single large space. In addition to the sleeping area in the back, there was a small, but useful kitchen area where they were now seated on either side of a table barely large enough for them both to eat at. He could see where it might be okay for one, but it was going to be way too cramped for two.

He said as much as they finished dinner. "How are we both going to live in this? It's way too small."

"We're not. This is just until the carnival moves on. You're going to have to stay here to deal with those men."

"But I ..."

"We can talk when I get back. The sun will be going down soon. The night is my best time. Stay here, or look around, I'll be back when we close."

"When's that?" Tim called to her back as she left the trailer.

"Eleven. Sooner if things are slow, but I don't think that will happen. It's a nice night." And then she was gone, on the way back to her tent. Tim was amazed that she could go back to work so soon after what had happened to her. Then he realized she had to work, that it was probably the only way she had to make any money.

Eleven? I can't sit here staring at these walls until eleven. I'll go crazy. I'm going to get out and walk around, get used to 1956.

When he left the trailer, he jumped the two feet to the ground, reveling in his rejuvenated body. His seventy-two-year-old self would have had to carefully negotiate each step to make sure he didn't slip and fall. He could get used to this real easy.

Except for the prizes in the games of chance, the midway he had seen the day before in 2006 had changed little from the one he saw now. It was the people who were going to take the most getting used to. For one thing, there wasn't a single person of color in the crowd. Vermont in 2006 wasn't a melting pot of the races, but in 1956 it appeared to be pure white bread. Apart from the clothes, it was the hair styles that jumped out at him. There wasn't a long-haired guy in the crowd, not even a teenager. Military haircuts were the norm here.

Then he realized something else that was *very* different. Some of the women passing by him were actually checking him out. The first time it happened he thought they must be looking at someone behind him. The second time he realized they were actually looking at him. He had to get used to being twenty-two years old again. Being six-foot-two and in pretty good shape didn't hurt either.

While he was strolling toward the Ferris wheel, he spotted one head that stuck out above the crowd. The man had red hair and a beard and was at least a foot taller than everyone surrounding him. This had to be the man who had raped Celeste. *The guy's got brass balls coming back here. Maybe I can find out who he is.*

Every carney at the fair stared daggers at the giant, and he seemed to revel in the attention. He undoubtedly knew what had happened when Celeste had reported the rape to the local police. The only reason he was here now was to flaunt it in the faces of the carnies. When Tim realized the man was slowly making his way toward Celeste's fortune-telling tent, he hustled to get there first. When Tim arrived there, she was already with a customer, so he took a seat on the bench outside. He'd only been sitting there a few minutes when he saw the giant's head bobbing above the crowd, coming his way.

One, two, three, four, five — five little groupies hanging on his coattails. Tim would bet dollars to donuts that he was looking at the assholes who had raped Celeste after Paul Bunyan had finished with her. Tim was terrible with names, but he had a thing for faces. He wouldn't forget any of these.

The customer inside the tent walked out just as the giant and his gang of five arrived. He turned and grinned at them, then started toward the entrance. Tim stood up, his pulse starting to race, and intercepted him. "Sorry, pal, I'm next. I've been waiting."

"I don't think so," the giant said. "Take a seat."

"Ah, nope. Like I said, I've been waiting. Why don't you take a seat?" Tim responded.

The giant clenched his fists, and it looked like they were going to have it out right there until one of the men with him grabbed one of the giant's arms and said something too low for Tim to hear. He didn't need to; Tim could see the crowd of carnies gathering in the midway behind the giant and his boys. The man gave Tim a look that could kill, then turned and stalked away. His crew trailed along behind him like a bunch of chicks following a momma hen.

When Tim turned to go into the tent, Celeste was standing in the entrance; she was shaking. "Don't worry, he'll never touch you again," he told her.

That night, as Tim and Celeste slept in her trailer, armed carnies stood watch outside.

The next day was a Monday, breakdown day. By afternoon, the entire troupe, including Celeste, was ready to be on the road to the next town. Tim was torn; he wanted to travel with them, but he had work to do here.

"How will I find you when I've done what I have to do here?"

"I don't know. I have a schedule of fairs we'll be doing from now until October. Then we head south for the winter. In the spring, we'll work our way north again."

"Will you be coming back here?"

"Of course. We do the Barkham Fair on the second weekend in July every year."

"Then I guess I'll see you then."

Celeste nodded and handed him an envelope. Tim looked inside and saw it was stuffed with bills. "You didn't have to …"

"I didn't. Well, some of it I did, but most of it is from the carnies. They took up a collection. It should be enough to hold you over until you can find a job." Tim just nodded and stuck it in his pocket. He'd count it later, after she was gone. "Burn each card when you've done what you must do. I'll know when you do."

The last thing she did before she left was kiss him. Once again, Tim felt a spark jump between them. Before she turned and walked away, she handed him another tarot card — The Dreamer. This one was hand-made and didn't appear to have come from the same deck as the others. The Fool was asleep on the ground, the white dog at his side. Above him, a woman dressed as a gypsy was asleep on a cloud. "Meet me in your dreams. I'll be waiting for you."

As he watched the caravan of cars, trucks, and trailers leave, Tim felt an overwhelming sense of loss. He had only been with Celeste for two days, but he wasn't sure he could live without her. Then some of the frustration that living in 1956 was going to cause hit him. Back in 2006, he could find her with the click of a few keys on a computer. He could call her on a cell phone anytime he wanted to talk to her. She would never be more than an instant away. Not here. Here, she might as well be in Timbuktu ... or on the moon.

* * *

After the troupe was gone, Tim opened the envelope Celeste had given him. *Jesus, two-hundred and twelve dollars! That's a fortune! This will carry me for quite a while, but not a year. I need a job. But first I need a place to live.*

During his walk to town, doubts filled his head. Could he really kill six men in cold blood, because that was really what she was asking him to do? There was no way he could get to one of them, make him suffer and tell him why, and then let him run off to warn the others. No. If he was going to do this, they had to die. He wasn't sure he could do that.

The walk into town was longer than Tim thought it would be. The Walmart and the Home Depot were gone. So were McDonald's and Burger King. Where they had been was open farmland. Barkham, when he reached it, was different, too. In his day, downtown had been in decline; people would rather shop at Walmart or Home Depot, where parking was easy and the prices were low. The downtown Tim was seeing now was the center of life in Barkham. The five-block, single Main Street was lined with three-story brick buildings. Storefronts filled the first level while office space or apartments occupied the second and third floors. What seemed like classic cars to him were either parked or driving up and down the street. The old F.W. Woolworth building was actually an F.W. Woolworth's. He couldn't remember the last time he had seen one of those. As he stepped closer to get a look through the big plate glass window, he noticed the "Help Wanted" sign in the lower, left-hand corner. Next to it was an "Apartment for Rent" sign. *Outstanding,* he thought, and went inside to inquire about the job and the apartment.

He wasn't in the store more than a few minutes before a man in a white shirt and a tie approached him. "Can I help you, sir?"

"Yes. I saw the Help Wanted sign in the window. I'd like to talk to someone about it."

The man looked him over and, despite Tim's outfit — he had been wearing the same clothes for three days, decided to take a chance on him. "It's a stock boy's position, but you'd be doing anything that needed to be done. That would include sweeping and cleaning up after the store closes. It's forty hours a week. The pay is minimum wage, a dollar an hour. You still interested?"

The man must have expected him to say, "No thanks," because he had a surprised look on his face when Tim answered, "Yes, sir."

"Good, when can you start?"

"Just as soon as I find a place to live and buy some clothes. I lost mine three days ago at the bus station in St. Johnsbury. I put my stuff down and went to get a sandwich. When I came back, everything was gone."

"That's terrible. Did you report it to the police?"

"No, it wasn't worth it. Besides, I wanted to keep moving. Then I saw the fair. I got a job there until they packed up and moved. So here I am."

"Well, you're in luck. There's a furnished apartment for rent upstairs, and you can buy anything else you'll need right here."

"Sounds like a deal. Who do I talk to about the room?"

"Me. I own the store and the building. Let me get you the keys. If you like the apartment, it's fifteen dollars a week, utilities included."

"If it's got a bed, a dresser, and a shower, I'll take it. Oh, and heat in the winter."

"It's not fancy, but it's got all those and then some."

"Then I'll take it. Now point me in the direction of the Men's Department so I can get some new clothes."

"Why don't I show you the apartment first?"

"Okay, let's do that. Then I'll have a place to take everything when I'm done shopping."

"Fine. Wait here and I'll get the keys."

The man was back within minutes. "By the way,

I'm Travis Meek. You can call me Mister Meek at work. Otherwise, it's Travis."

"Oh, Tim Ritter," Tim answered, and offered Meek his hand.

"Now then, let's go see that apartment," Meek told him, and led him outside to a door tucked in an alcove at the side of the store. He showed Tim a ring with three keys on it. "The big one's for the front door. Never leave it unlocked. We trust people around here, but not that much. Remember what happened to you in St. Johnsbury."

Tim followed Meek up one flight of stairs, and then another, to the third floor, where there were four apartments. The second key on the ring unlocked 3C. After opening the door, Meek led Tim inside and handed him the keys. "What's this one for?" Tim asked, holding out the third key on the ring out to Meek.

"That's for the back door. There's a parking lot in the rear of the building."

"Good to know," Tim answered, and pocketed the keys.

"Well, this is it. Look around and get an idea of what you'll need."

After Meek left, Tim took a quick tour of his new digs. The room he had entered off the hall was a combination kitchen/living room. The kitchen half contained a small stove, a refrigerator, a sink, and a few cabinets and drawers. Inside those he found plates and utensils for two, a percolator-style coffee pot, and a few pots and pans. An old, but serviceable couch, a floor lamp, and an end table filled the living room side.

In the bedroom, Tim found a full-sized bed, a dresser with four drawers, a bedside table, and a closet.

The bed and pillows were stripped. He was going to have to buy sheets and pillowcases. The bathroom was off this room. It contained a toilet, a sink, a small wall-mounted medicine cabinet, and a standup shower with a plastic curtain.

This will do fine, he thought. Then he went back to the store to do some much-needed shopping.

Tim found everything he needed in Woolworth's — two pairs of pants, two white shirts, a tie, black socks, toiletries, sheets, pillowcases, a blanket for the bed, and a cheap alarm clock to replace the digital watch he had to destroy. That was enough to get him started. He was on his way to the cashier when he noticed a deck of tarot cards and a beginner's book for reading them. He added both to the pile.

When he went to the cashier, Meek was waiting for him. "Tim, this is Estelle Fuller. Estelle, Tim Ritter. Starting tomorrow, Tim's going to be working with us, so give him the employee discount. Every little bit helps, right, Tim?"

"Right," Tim agreed. Then, before Meek could leave, he asked, "What time do you want me to start tomorrow?"

"Be here at eight and we'll fill out the paperwork. The store doesn't open 'til nine. Just knock on the door and I'll let you in."

When Tim turned back to Estelle, she gave him a bright smile, followed by a puzzled look. "Starting tomorrow? That was quick."

Tim guessed Estelle Fuller to be in her forties. She was short, maybe five-five, a little overweight, nice looking, but not beautiful. The ring on her left hand told him she was married. Five days ago he would have thought of her as young. Now he had to adjust his thinking; she was probably twenty years older than he was.

"I needed a job and this one was the first thing I saw."

"Well, I hope you like it." Then she lowered her voice to a whisper. "I hope you stay. We have trouble keeping people."

"Really, why?" Tim asked.

"Minimum wage. As soon as they find something that pays better, they leave."

Tim thought about that before answering. This job sounded like what he needed for now: regular hours, a place to live upstairs, and a chance to meet a lot of people. Hopefully that would include the five who had tagged along behind the giant. "I think this will do me just fine," he finally answered.

Once he was back in his room and had showered and changed clothes, Tim had time to think about the last thing Meek had said: paperwork. That could be a problem until he once again realized *when* he was. No computers, no real checks. He'd just fill it out with his real information. Easy peasy. ID was going to be the problem. Everything he had was from 2006. He could hardly pull out a driver's license that expired in 2008 with an old man's picture on it. Once he was settled, though, he could write to Jersey for a new birth certificate and driver's license.

What now? Tim thought once he had settled in. *I can't just sit here looking at these walls all night. No TV, no computer, no internet. I'll go crazy if I don't do something.*

When his stomach growled, he realized he hadn't eaten since breakfast with Celeste. *Okay, dinner. That should waste an hour.*

He found a family-style restaurant, "Annie's Place,"

a block down from Woolworth's. When he opened the door and went in, he was greeted by a waitress in a white uniform with "Alice" embroidered over her left breast. "Would you like a booth or a table?" she asked with a smile.

Tim smiled back. "I'll take a booth." He wanted the privacy.

Alice led him to a booth and placed a menu on the table. "I'll be back to take your order in a minute. Can I bring you something to drink when I do?"

"Coffee. Decaf would be nice."

"I don't have brewed decaf. You want instant?"

Instant? Yuck! "No thanks. Just black coffee will be fine." He almost asked for Sweet 'n Low before noticing there was only sugar on the table.

Alice was back a minute later with his coffee and a smile. "Ready to order, or do you need a few more minutes?"

"No, I'm ready. I'll have the meatloaf and mashed potatoes with gravy. What's the vegetable?"

"Corn."

"Okay, corn."

"You want gravy on the potatoes, too?"

"Yes, please."

"You got it," Alice said and went to place the order.

Annie's turned out to be a good place to eat until he could do some shopping and get organized. The service was friendly, the food good, and it was close to his apartment.

When Tim finished his meal, he checked the bill, left a ten-percent tip on the table, and went to the front to pay the cashier. Then, just as he stepped outside, he saw a face he recognized from the group that had been with the giant. The man it belonged to was wearing a Texaco shirt. *Hubie* was written under the familiar Red Star logo. As he walked outside, an old advertising jingle jumped into his head: *You can trust your car to the man who wears the star. The big red Texaco star.*

Maybe you can trust your car to him, Tim thought, *but not your daughter.*

After he left Annie's, it was still too early to go back and sit in an empty apartment, so he decided to take a walk and explore downtown Barkham, vintage 1956. Many of these storefronts would be empty in 2006, and even more would be occupied by different businesses. One that caught his eye was Pete's Barber Shop. An old fashioned red-and-white barber's pole hung from the building outside the shop. When he peered in through the window, he saw two barber's chairs, four chairs for customers to sit in while they waited to get a cut, and the requisite table filled with well-worn magazines that were probably months old. Wildroot and Brylcreem posters hung on the walls. Pete's was long gone in 2006. It had been replaced by Supercuts and styling salons outside of town.

Tim returned to the apartment just after the sun went down. The walk up two flights of stairs to the third floor reminded him of just how much walking he had done that day. Before he did anything else, he looked through the beginner's book on tarot for the card Celeste had given him before she left — The Dreamer. It wasn't in the book, and it wasn't in the deck of cards. She must have made it just for him.

After a hot shower that felt great on his aching muscles, Tim was ready for a good night's sleep. He set the alarm for six the next morning and was asleep within minutes of his head hitting the pillow.

Tim's sleep was not dreamless. Instead, it was filled with the terror Celeste had felt when the giant had snatched her out of her bed and carried her into the woods. In his dream, he was Celeste. The big man ripped off his clothes and slammed him to the ground. Pain shot through his back, but it paled in comparison to the pain and humiliation he felt when the giant pried his legs open and forced himself into him. He was only inside him for a minute or two before he climbed off him and turned him over to the five men who had been waiting for their turn at him. When they were done, he lay torn and battered on the forest floor.

Tim awoke with a start, the nightmare fresh in his mind. Any doubts he had about killing the assholes who had raped Celeste were gone. It took him a long time to fall back asleep. When he did, this time it was deep and dreamless.

* * *

Celeste also awoke with a start. Reliving the rape had been horrible, but knowing that Tim had had to share it with her was the worst part. How could he stand to look at her after seeing that? She would have spared him that if she could. She knew it wouldn't be the last time she'd have that nightmare. It would plague her as long as the men who had raped her still lived.

Chapter Eight

Hubie Martin had just taken a bite of his tuna salad sandwich when a car pulled up to the pumps outside and the *ding-ding* of the alarm bell chimed. Hubie hated that damn bell. It went off every time someone drove over the black cable that ran from the gas pumps to the office. He'd rip the damn thing out if he could, but the owner would have a fit. "Shit," he swore, and put the sandwich down. "Five minutes. That's all I want is five fucking minutes to eat in peace. Is that too much to ask?"

Hubie had to keep from swearing again when he saw the car that was waiting at the pump — Annabelle Pendleton's '48 Dodge. As if interrupting his dinner wasn't enough, Annabelle was going to buy three gallons of regular. That's all she ever bought and always had exact change: three quarters, a dime, and a nickel. And shame on him if he went a penny over, or a penny under, on the pump.

"Hello, Hubie, I'll have three gallons, please," the old biddy told him through her open window.

"Yea, ma'am. Can I check your oil, too?"

"No, but don't forget the windshield. The bugs are terrible this time of year."

"Yes, ma'am," Hubie answered on his way to pump the gas. When he was done, he gave himself a mental pat on the back for getting it exactly right. If he had gone under, she would have insisted he keep pumping. If he had gone over, she would have refused to pay the extra and he would have had to make up the difference. He got the squeegee to clean her windshield and went around to the front of the car. *Bugs my ass. There isn't a bug on here. But I can't tell her that. She'll just insist there are. Better to just clean it.*

It took all of five minutes to pump the gas and clean the windshield. When he got back to his sandwich, a fly had landed on it. His sandwich was ruined. He couldn't eat anything that a fly had been on. "God damn it!" Hubie swore. Now he was going to have to stop at Annie's if he wanted dinner tonight. It was that, or tell his wife he had thrown his sandwich out because of a fly. He'd never hear the end of that. There were two things she just couldn't understand — his obsession with flies, and his hero worship — her words — of Stu Miller. He'd just tell her he had to stay late.

He was just about to open the door to Annie's when it swung open and almost hit him. When he stepped back, a stranger walked out. He met the man's eyes and had the distinct feeling he'd seen him before. Maybe he had stopped at the station for gas.

Chapter Nine

The alarm went off at 6:00 a.m., the dream as vivid in his mind then as it had been when he woke in the night. He tried to put it out of his head, but it was impossible. Nevertheless, he was up, showered, and dressed by 6:20. At 6:30 he realized he had forgotten to put toilet paper on his list. Luckily, it was before he sat down. A short walk took him to Annie's, where he took care of that problem.

Coming out of the men's room, he searched in his pocket for a dime to buy a newspaper before realizing he had left his change on the bedside table.

"Can you make change for a buck?" he asked the waitress. "I want to get a paper,"

"Sure, glad to," she answered, and punched the open key on the cash register. No Sale popped up in the little window on top and the drawer opened with a ding Tim hadn't heard in years. The woman dug out three quarters, two dimes, and a nickel and handed them to

Tim as he passed her the dollar. "You want to order now, or wait till you get your paper?"

"I can do it now. I'll have a bacon and cheese omelet, home fries, wheat toast, and coffee."

"You going to sit at the counter, or do you want a booth?"

"The counter will be fine," Tim answered, and went outside to get a paper from the box. He read it from cover to cover while eating, trying to catch up on what was happening in Vermont and the world. He was amazed at how much he didn't remember. It was like he had managed to skip 1956 entirely in his previous life.

Other things from that life stood out clear in his memory — John Kennedy's assassination, Bobby Kennedy and Martin Luther King, the fall of Saigon. He would experience all those again. This time the shock would be replaced by the foreknowledge that they would occur and that he could do nothing to stop them. Then he realized there were things in his past/future that could help him. Stocks like Amazon and IBM he could buy for a song that would soar in value, the year the Jets beat the Colts in the Super Bowl. Bucky Dent's home run in Fenway.

* * *

Tim tapped on the glass of Woolworth's front door at exactly eight o'clock. Mr. Meek appeared so quickly to unlock it that he knew the man had been waiting to see if he would arrive on time. *Okay, I passed the first test. Let's see how the rest of the day goes.*

Filling out the required paperwork took all of fifteen minutes. Tim explained that he didn't have his social security card with him, but he knew what it was. Driver's license? Nope, never had one. He filled out a form for his taxes, and that was it. The rest of the morning was spent learning where everything in the store was. He had a half hour off for lunch, which he spent eating an egg salad sandwich with lettuce and tomato on a hard roll at the lunch counter. He was done for the day at 4:30 and faced another night of staring at the walls. He thought of buying a book, but then had a better idea. If he was going to deal with Celeste's attackers, and that's what he was here for, he had to get in better shape than he was now. He might not be able to get into the same shape he had been when he was an Army Ranger, but he could try.

Step one in the process was to get some good running shoes, some shorts, white socks, and a few tees. The shorts and tees were easy, the running shoes not so much. He had to settle for a pair of low-cut Converse sneakers. He wanted to get started right away, but first he needed to do some grocery shopping. He couldn't afford to eat every meal at Annie's.

The shopping took less than an hour because he quickly realized that he could only buy as much as he could carry. For right now he just needed the basics. That left him enough time for a good two-mile run.

Tim quickly realized that his two-mile run was going to turn into a one miler — if he was lucky. There was no rhythm to his stride, and he was sucking wind after half a mile. When he got back to his building, he stood bent over with his hands on his knees and a stitch in his side. *This sucks. I remember being in better shape than this.* Apparently, he was wrong. The mind was willing, but the muscle memory was gone.

Over the next week, Tim found out just how hard

it actually was getting started with only the clothes on his back. There were things he had taken for granted that he absolutely needed: a place to wash and dry his clothes, an ironing board and iron, a toaster, a radio to break the silence when he was sitting alone in his apartment, and a water bottle or something for his runs. And that was just the short list. The high point of his day was when he dreamt of Celeste after falling asleep each night.

It was two weeks before his evening run took him far enough to find the Texaco station. It was about a mile out of town. He could have just asked about it, but it would have seemed funny, a guy without a car asking about a gas station. As he approached it, he slowed, and then stopped when he was directly across from it. He stretched and took a sip of water as he studied it.

The station was right out of the fifties. He couldn't remember the building being there in 2006. There were two pumps outside, one for regular, the other for premium. A rack of oil cans stood between them. Half of the one-story, white cinder block building was dominated by a single roll-up door where cars were brought in for service. A door and a large plate glass window filled the other half. There was a man inside sitting at a desk, but Tim couldn't see his face clearly enough to identify him.

So, Hubie, is this where you work?

Tim was about to leave when the *ding-ding* of a car pulling in stopped him. A few seconds later the man who had been sitting behind the desk came out wiping his hands on a red shop rag. A quick glance was all Tim needed to know he had found his man. On his run back to the apartment, he tried to think

48

what he was going to do about it. Then he remembered what Celeste had said about the tarot cards. *Study them, let them talk to you. One card for each of the men with The Emperor. When each man's time comes, the cards will tell you what they want.*

Over the next three weeks, Tim struggled with what he was about to do. How would going down the path he was on change him? Could he take another life to save his own? Is that what he was doing? He had killed in Nam in his previous life, but he hadn't killed yet in this one. But this was different. After everything was said and done, that's what this all came down to, wasn't it? Six men had raped a young woman, and the police had blown her off. What was he going to do about it? Could he be judge and jury? Could he be Mike Hammer? No matter how many times he brought up the argument in his head, the answer was: Yes, he could. Not just for Celeste and Kristen, but for all the other women these guys might rape. Rapists don't stop. Celeste might not even have been the first. She definitely wouldn't be the last. How many more women would there be? How many more lives would they ruin? None, if he could help it. He had struggled for years to get over what he had done in Nam. Now he was thankful for the man he had been. If it hadn't been for those years, he could never do what he had to do now.

* * *

Tim spread the cards face down on his kitchen table in the same pentagram pattern Celeste had placed them in.

So, Hubie, which one of these are you? he thought, before reaching out and selecting the one on the upper right-hand side of the pattern. That one called to him. When he flipped it over, it revealed an armored warrior in a chariot flanked by black-and-white Egyptian lions. The Chariot.

The beginner's book of tarot reading he had bought along with a set of cards said The Fool meets The Charioteer late in his journey, but here he was meeting him at the beginning of his. It also said the card represented war and a victory over his adversaries. Did any of that matter? Celeste had told him the card would tell him what it wanted. *Don't worry about it, it'll come,* he thought, and then decided to treat himself to dinner at Annie's.

"Hi, Tim," Tina, the waitress on duty, greeted him when he took his normal seat in a booth across from the counter. He didn't come in all that often, but he and Tina had struck up a budding friendship during the times he had come in.

Tim's dinner had just arrived when a man wearing a police uniform walked in. He looked around the restaurant before taking a seat at the counter across from Tim's booth. Tina approached him as soon as he was seated. "Evening, Sheriff. You here for dinner, or just coffee?"

"Dinner. I'll have the special, whatever it is."

"You sure? It's the Fisherman's Platter."

"In that case, I'll have a rib eye and a baked potato."

Tim grinned when he heard that. He had snapped up the Fisherman's Platter when Tina told him it was the special. He hadn't had a good old-fashioned plateful of fried food in ages. All that healthy eating, and he had still gotten cancer.

He doubted the sheriff was a health nut. That shit wouldn't start for another twenty years or so. *I guess he's just an old-fashioned meat-and-potatoes kind of guy. Just like I was. Enjoy it while you can, sheriff. Forty years from now, they're going to be telling you red meat is a killer.*

While the sheriff was waiting for his dinner, he spun around on his stool and caught Tim looking at him. He nodded and Tim nodded back. "You new in town, or just passing through?"

"I'm new here," Tim answered.

"Well, then welcome. I'm Sheriff Miller."

"Tim Ritter."

"Nice to meet you, Tim. What brings you to Barkham?"

"Looking for someplace a little less hectic than New Jersey. I always heard Vermont was nice, so I took a bus up here to see for myself. I like it, so I decided to stay." Everything was true except for the bus part. Jersey had changed so much between the time he went in the army and the time he got out that it didn't feel like home when he came back. And there were too many memories of Kristen there.

When the sheriff's dinner came, he spun back around to face it, and something in the way he looked, or the way he moved, struck Tim as familiar. It gnawed at him the entire time he was eating. He didn't realize what it was until he was back in his apartment. Put a beard on the guy, change his hair from blond to red, and make him six inches taller and he could be Paul Bunyan's brother. That could explain why the police had blown Celeste off when she tried to report the rape.

* * *

Tim waited, carried the card in his pocket for days, but it never spoke to him. Then, during a five-mile run, when his mind was wandering, it came to him.

Tim's work schedule was pretty steady. He worked from Tuesday to Saturday with Sunday and Monday off. Sometimes Meek asked him to work on a Monday, but it was never on an overtime basis. If Tim worked Monday, he got Tuesday off. He could see why Estella had said people usually found a higher-paying job and moved on.

On this Monday, Tim was perched on a stump across from the Texaco station with a pad and pencil. He'd also been there on Sunday, but Hubie apparently had Sunday off, too. Today, he had two questions to answer. First, was the station a one-man operation, and second, was there a slow period when he could get at Hubie without anyone interrupting them?

As he watched, he got a feel for what an asshole Hubie was. Sometimes, when a car drove in, the man would sit at his desk for no other reason than to make the customer wait. Sometimes he would flip them the bird after they had driven away. Tim could see this guy taking his turn in a gang rape. He was making it easy for him to justify what he was planning.

* * *

Hubie Martin came out from under the '51 Studebaker Commander he was doing an oil change on and closed the roll-up door to the service bay. He'd let the oil drain while he was eating lunch and finish the job when he was done. As he walked through the connecting door to the office, he never saw the man who jumped out of the woods and was sprinting toward the station.

Just as Hubie was about to lock the front door and flip the OPEN/CLOSED sign to CLOSED, a man wearing shorts, a tee-shirt, and sneakers burst through the door. "Hey, I'm closing for lunch. Come back in half an hour."

"Don't worry, this won't take long," the man answered.

"You're right, it won't. Come back in half an hour."

Hubie didn't even have time to be amazed when the man suckered punched him in the stomach. As he doubled over from the blow, the guy slipped around him and got him in a choke hold. He struggled, but it did no good; the man was strong and knew what he was doing. In a minute, Hubie's world turned gray, then black.

He was being dragged across the floor toward the service bay when he started to regain consciousness. "What …" he mumbled, then an arm went around his neck and the black returned.

The next time he awoke, he was lying flat on his back, pinned under the Studebaker. The transmission was crushing his chest and oil was dripping onto his face and into his eyes. He turned his head away from the drip only to have it start to fill his ear. Then there was a man's voice he didn't recognize. "Good, you're back. Now we can talk."

"Who are you?" Hubie wheezed, the weight on his chest making it hard to talk.

"Doesn't matter."

"What do you want?"

"Better question. Do you remember the woman you and your friends raped at the Barkham Fair? Do you think this was how she felt when you laid on top of her?"

Oh shit, oh shit, Hubie thought, but managed to wheeze out, "No."

"One more chance, Hubie. Lie to me again and the Stude comes all the way down. Tell me what I want to know and I'll let you go. I only want the big guy."

"Man, you don't want to mess with him. He'll kill you."

"I'll take my chances," the man said. "Now what's his name?"

"Stu Miller."

"Good. Now, who were the other four?"

"You said you only wanted the big guy."

"You want to die for them, Hubie?" the man asked when he didn't give up the names.

"No. It was Sawyer Gaunt, Bill Burke, Bucky St. John, and Jack Baker."

"See, that wasn't so hard, was it?"

"No, now let me out," Hubie wheezed.

"Sorry, Hubie, if I do that, you're going to run straight to that big fucker and, like you said, he'll kill me. I can't let that happen."

"Wait! You said you'd let me go if I told you what you wanted to know."

"I lied," the stranger answered.

"Wait! Wait!" Hubie tried to scream, but it came out as a squeak. Then he heard the lift's hydraulic cylinder hiss. An instant later the pressure on his chest became unbearable. He actually heard his ribs crack. The pain was overwhelming. The car didn't drop enough to crush him, just enough to make it impossible to breathe.

Oh my god! Oh my god! Please let me out! Please don't do this! Hubie tried to beg, but nothing came out. He heard the man open and close the front door on his way out. After that, the gray, then the black, returned. And after that, nothing.

* * *

"I lied," Tim told him. Hubie was squealing, trying to beg Tim to stop. He had one last chance to step away from this path, and then thought, *Like Celeste begged you not to rape her?* He let the lift holding the Studebaker come all the way down. It didn't squash Hubie like the bug he was, but it was enough to crush his chest. Surprisingly, he felt no remorse. In fact, it felt good. He hadn't been able to do anything when Kristen was raped. It had haunted him for years. This was a little payback for her, too.

He waited until there was no traffic on the road before starting his run home. He had been running this route every day for weeks. Anyone who saw him would be used to him by now. It was just good luck that no one drove past before he was well into town.

When he got back to his apartment, he touched a match to The Chariot card. It burst into a weird green flame and was gone almost before he could drop it. The next time he would be more careful.

* * *

In North Hampton, Celeste felt the heat from its burning and knew one of her rapists was dead. The darkness that had surrounded her since she had left Barkham lightened just a bit. Which one was gone? She didn't know. She would find that out later.

The dreamers met in their sleep. Tim relived his

encounter with Hubie Martin. Celeste experienced it with him. She was there when Tim positioned Hubie under the lift and lowered the Studebaker onto his chest to pin him in place. She heard Hubie give up the names of the big man and the others and she pulled the lever that allowed the car to drop the rest of the way onto Hubie's chest. When she woke, she burst into tears. She knew Tim had felt no remorse over what he had done, but she couldn't say the same. She felt nothing for the rapist; her tears were for Tim.

Later, after she fell asleep, they dreamed of the rape. This time Hubie Martin was missing.

* * *

Millie Martin went to bed pissed when Hubie still wasn't home at eleven. *I warned him. If he's out drinking with Stu Miller and the rest of his friends, I'm leaving him. We agreed that once a month is enough.*

After two years of marriage, Hubie's hero worship of Stu Miller was wearing thin. She'd known Hubie was friends with Stu when they got married, but she'd thought Hubie would break away from him once they had tied the knot. It hadn't happened. Any time Stu called, Hubie would still jump and run. She'd laid down the law the night he came home from the Barkham Fair at three in the morning. He could still have his night out on the third Thursday of the month to be with Stu and the boys at Kelly's, but that was it. Rolling in drunk at two o'clock in the morning once a month was more than enough.

When Millie woke up at six the next morning and Hubie still wasn't home, her anger turned to concern.

* * *

Amy Swift wasn't even through the door and the phone was already ringing. "Barkham Police," she said when she picked it up, hoping the caller was still there.

"Hello? This is Millie Martin. My husband never came home from work last night and I'm worried about him. He's never done this before."

"I'm sure there must be a reason for it Missus Martin, but I'll let you talk to Sheriff Miller," Amy told her.

Amy put Millie on hold and paged Cole on the intercom. "Sheriff, Millie Martin's on the line. She say's Hubie never came home last night. She wants to talk to you."

What did they do now? Miller thought as he reached for the phone. "Morning, Millie. Amy says Hubie didn't come home last night?"

"That's right. He's never done this before. He comes home late sometimes, but he always comes home."

"I'm sure he's okay, Millie. But I'll check around, okay?"

"Okay. Thank you, Sheriff."

"No problem, but if he calls or comes home, please let us know."

"I will, and thanks again," Millie said before hanging up.

* * *

The first thing Cole did was call his brother. "Pick up, Stu," he said into the phone after the tenth ring. Stu finally did on the fourteenth.

"What?" his brother grumbled on the other end.

"Millie Martin called me. Hubie never made it home last night. Were you guys out partying?"

"You woke me up for that?"

"Just answer the question. Was Hubie with you last night?"

"No."

"Any idea where he might be?"

"No, and I'm not his fucking nursemaid. Maybe he just got tired of Millie's shit and decided not to go back."

"Maybe," Cole agreed, but he didn't think so. Hubie didn't have the balls for it.

After he hung up, Cole decided to take a ride out to the Texaco station and see if Hubie had shown up at work.

Good, he's here, Cole thought when he saw Hubie's car parked next to the station. *I'd better go inside and see what's going on.*

When Cole saw all the lights on inside the station and the CLOSED sign in the window, he had a feeling something was wrong. When he pushed the door and it swung open, he really got concerned. "Hubie?" he called, but got no answer.

Next, he went into the service bay. Except for a Studebaker, the bay was empty. He was about to leave when he saw a foot sticking out from under the back of the car. "Ah, shit," he swore as he got down on his knees to get a better look.

I'd better call Amy and get her to send an ambulance out here to get him, Cole thought. He made the call from the office phone so all the idiots with police scanners wouldn't be on the phone or driving out to the station before Amy could even make the call.

Unlike his brother, Amy picked up on the second ring. "Barkham Police Department," she answered in a pleasant voice.

"Amy, this is Cole. I need you to send an ambulance out to the Texaco station. Tell Ted to come out, too. Hubie Martin had an accident. He's dead. There's no rush, so tell them no lights or sirens. As soon as Ted's here, I'll go over and talk to Millie."

While he waited for Swanson and the ambulance to arrive, Cole raised the lift to get it off Hubie. *Bad luck,* he thought. *The transmission came down right on his chest.*

* * *

Ted Swanson arrived at the station minutes before the ambulance. "Aw, man," Ted said when he saw Hubie's body on the floor.

"Yeah," Cole agreed. "You take over here. Have them take the body to Wills' Funeral Home. I'm going over to talk to his wife."

"Better you than me," Swanson told him, and then went to meet the guys from the ambulance.

* * *

On the drive to Hubie's house, Cole wondered how he was going to break the news to his wife. *Better just come right out and tell her*, he thought as he walked up to the door to ring the bell.

Millie Martin's face fell when she saw the Sheriff at the door. "What happened? Is he all right?"

"I'm sorry, Millie. There was an accident at the station. He got caught under a car he was working on.

Hubie's ... well, Hubie's dead."

It took a second for the shock of what he had just told her to sink in. Then Millie collapsed in his arms.

Chapter Ten

When Stu strolled into Kelley's Bar, he was annoyed to see that Hubie Martin wasn't there yet. *I'm going to have to talk to that boy. He knows I'm always the last one to get here. I don't wait for anyone.*

"Where's Hubie?" he demanded when he sat down in his normal seat at the table.

"You didn't hear?" Baker asked.

"Hear what?"

"Hubie's dead."

"Bullshit. Don't fuck around with me."

"No lie," Sawyer Gaunt told him. "He got caught under the lift at the garage. It crushed his chest."

"Man, that sucks. When did it happen?"

"Monday," Bill Burke told him.

"Monday? Today's Thursday. Why the hell am I just hearing about this now?"

The four men in the group looked at each other, but no one said anything.

"Well, fuck it. Somebody get a pitcher and we'll

drink to him."

Jack Baker was the closest to the bar, so he got up to get it. When he came back, he set the pitcher in front of Stu. The big man grabbed it and poured himself a beer. Stu always got the first glass, and the last one, out of a pitcher. It was one of many of the unspoken rules they lived by.

Once everyone had filled their glass, Stu raised his and offered the toast. "To Hubie."

"To Hubie," they all agreed and clinked glasses.

Stu was pouring his second glass when Missy stopped by the table, careful to keep out of the reach of his arm. If she got too close, he'd grab a bit of ass when she turned to leave. "You guys want the usual? Two large pepperoni and sausage?"

"Yeah, and another pitcher," Stu told her.

Stu watched her ass twitch and laughed as she walked away with the order. He knew she'd have to get close enough for a quick feel when she brought the next pitcher of beer. Someday he was going to get *more* than a quick feel — whether she liked it or not.

When she was gone, Stu turned his attention back to his crew. "So, who found the body?"

Jack Baker answered, "Your brother. Millie called him when Hubie didn't come home. Cole went over there and found the CLOSED sign on the door, but it was unlocked and all the lights were on. When he went into the service bay, he found Hubie under the Stude that was on the lift."

"How the hell did that happen?"

"Nobody knows. Hubie worked alone."

Stu saw Bucky St. John eyeing the pitcher. There was just enough in it to fill one more glass, and Bucky's was empty. Stu's was still half full, but he held off on finishing it just to make Bucky squirm. *You'd better not reach for that pitcher, Bucky. You know what will happen if you do.*

When Missy brought the new pitcher, she placed it on the table and tried to skip away before Stu could grab her ass. She wasn't fast enough, and he got a good feel.

Stu downed the last of his beer and reached for the new pitcher. "Go ahead and finish that one, Bucky. We'll start on this one."

When the first pizza came, the guy who brought it placed it in the middle of the table. Stu gave him an annoyed look, then slid the pan closer before taking the first slice. After he had his, the others each took one. That left three slices.

Stu finished his slice and reached for a second. Once he had it, Sawyer and Bill were free to take another one.

When the second pizza came, Stu once again took the first slice, then ordered a third pitcher of beer. This time when Missy brought it, Stu had his head turned and she managed to leave the pitcher and skip out of reach before Stu could cop another feel.

"Hubie's wake is tomorrow at Wills' Funeral Home at six. I'm going to stop in and pay my respects. How about you guys?" Gaunt asked.

Baker, St. John, and Burke all said they would, then looked expectantly at Stu. "Maybe. I hate those things."

Stu and the boys went through two more pitchers, using the excuse of toasting Hubie's memory. Stu drank at least one of them himself. When he got up to leave, he dropped a five on the table, leaving the guys to cover the rest.

Once he was out of Kelly's, Stu staggered a bit on

the way to his pickup. He was truly drunk. *No problem. There isn't a cop in this town who would dare stop me.* Then he thought about Hubie and got pissed. *Stupid shit. Now I'm going to have to pay someone to work on my truck.*

* * *

Baker was the first to arrive at the funeral home at 6:30. He stood outside waiting for the others before going in. Burke and St. John got there at 6:45. Gaunt was the last to show up at 6:50. "Well, we're all here. You think Stu's going to show?" he asked when he joined them.

"Maybe," St. John answered. "Who knows? He said he hated these things, so we might as well go in."

The men walked in as a group. The reception room wasn't filled, but there were people there from both sides of Hubie's family. His wife, Millie, was greeting guests as they arrived. Each of the men stopped to say a few words before taking a seat at the back of the room, where they were pretty much ignored by the rest of the mourners.

Stu walked in at 7:50. Unlike the other men who were in suits and a tie, he was dressed in jeans, boots, and a short-sleeved shirt that showed off his biceps. Millie Martin frowned when she saw him and refused to acknowledge his presence. Stu ignored her, too. He just walked to the coffin, took a quick glance inside, then turned to survey the room. When he saw his crew seated in the back, he nodded to them before walking back out.

When the guys went outside, they expected to see Stu waiting for them. He was nowhere to be seen.

None of them attended the funeral the next day.

Chapter Eleven

Tim had the names, now he just had to find the men who went with them. The first thing he had to do was decide *who* he was going to deal with next. Not Stu Miller, that was for sure. He was going to leave him for last. He wanted Stu to know he was coming.

How about you, Bucky St. John?

Once again Tim spread the cards face down and picked one. When he flipped it over, it was a horned devil flanked by a naked man and woman — The Devil. Tim laughed. He got the joke. Now all he had to do was find the man.

Damn, I wish I had the internet. I could just look him up. Wait, maybe I can. All I need is a phone book. There's one by the pay phone at the back of the store.

* * *

Jesus, how many damn St. John's are there in this town?

Tim thought when he looked up the name in the white pages. When he counted, there were thirteen. Not one of them was a Bucky. *Right, it's a nickname.* From the look of the addresses, they were all over town. *That's going to complicate things, especially since I don't have a car.* Tim looked around, didn't see anyone, and started to tear the page from the book. Then a better idea struck him. He'd just call each number and ask for Bucky.

Tim put a dime in the phone, heard it ding as it dropped through, then dialed the first number.

"Hello?"

"Hello, may I speak to Bucky, please?"

There was a moment of silence on the other end before an icy male voice replied, "Wrong number, pal, and if you're a friend of Bucky's, don't call back." Then the line went dead.

Whoa, Bucky, somebody doesn't like you very much.

Tim got similar results on the next three calls. On the fifth, he got lucky. "This is Bucky, who's this?"

"John Peters," Tim answered.

"Never heard of you. What do you want?"

"I heard you've got an old Chevy pickup for sale. I was wondering if I could get a look at it?"

"I think you heard wrong. I don't have a pickup. Never did."

"Sorry ..." Tim started to say, but he was already talking to a dead line.

Oh, Bucky, you are an asshole. I'm looking forward to meeting you. Now I just have to find 79 Ringwood Avenue.

He was tempted to go after St. John now, but it was too soon after Hubie. He'd give it a month. For now, he'd settle for finding out all he could about the man.

The next day at work, Tim asked Estella if she

knew where Ringwood Avenue was. "Ringwood Avenue? What would you want to go out there for?"

"I don't. I just heard someone mention it, and I never saw it on any of my runs, so I was wondering where it was."

"It's out past the fair grounds. It's nothing more than a dirt road with a bunch of mobile homes and run-down houses. You don't want to go running out there."

"Thanks, Stell. It doesn't sound like any place I'll be going soon." But it was, on his next day off.

* * *

Ringwood Avenue was just as Estella said it was — a dirt road with mobile homes and run-down shacks. Every one of them had a German Shepherd or a Rottweiler tied up outside that barked and strained at its chain when Tim ran past.

Jesus, I'm a dead man if one of them gets loose.

The address he was looking for turned out to be shit-box trailer with a rusted-out '48 Pontiac up on blocks in a weed-infested side yard. A newer '52 Buick sat in front of the trailer. The required mutt, this one a pit bull, was poking its head out of a squat dog house that looked as worn as the trailer. As soon as it saw Tim, it shot out of its house, barking and growling, streaking toward him until its chain brought it to a jolting stop. It continued to bark and strain on its chain until a man opened the door of the trailer and yelled at it to shut the fuck up. After seeing him, there was no doubt in Tim's mind that he was one of Miller's crew.

On the run back to the main road, Tim couldn't

see any way of getting to St. John in his trailer. The entire length of Ringwood Avenue was an intruder alert system of barking dogs. It was like the guy was in a damn fortress. He was going to have to find another way, but how?

After three weeks of racking his brain, Tim was no closer to finding a way to get to St. John than he had been on that first day. The problem was consuming him. It must have been apparent because Estella confronted him on his way out of work one night. "Tim, what's bothering you? You look like somebody who lost his best friend, or someone who needs one. Do you ever do anything besides run after work?"

"Sure."

"Like what?"

"I exercise, lift weights ... lots of things."

"Tim, you've been here for two months. You've got to get out, have some fun, meet people."

"How do you suggest I do that?"

"Why not go to church? You could meet people that way."

Tim almost laughed. "I'm not a church kind of guy. Never have been. Any other ideas?"

Estella gave him a stony look before sharing her next suggestion. "Well, Kelly's Pub has a two-for-one night on the third Thursday of each month — two beers for the price of one, two pizzas for the price of one between five and six o'clock. Then they have live music at seven."

"Stell, I couldn't eat one pizza, so what would I do with two?"

"You don't go to eat the pizza; you go to have a little fun. You should try it. It's this week, you know."

"I'll think about it," Tim promised.

* * *

"You going to Kelly's tonight?" Estella asked when she arrived for work Thursday morning.

"Maybe. I haven't given it much thought."

"Just go. Have some fun."

She mentioned it at least once an hour for the rest of the day. Tim finally asked her why it was so important to her.

"Because I like you. You've already lasted more than most of the help we get. I don't want you to get depressed and quit."

"Fine, I'll go," he finally promised just to make her happy, but she still reminded him about it on his way out the door at 4:30.

"I'm going. I'm going," he assured her, and then went upstairs to change into jeans and a flannel shirt.

I'm going to have to get a jacket soon, Tim thought on his walk over to Kelly's. It was late September, and the leaves were already turning in Vermont. It would still be a few weeks before they started to change in Jersey. *I wonder where Celeste is right now?*

Tim got to Kelly's just after five. He took a seat at the bar and ordered a beer. "Bud on tap, okay?" the bartender asked.

"Bud's fine."

"It's happy hour, two for one between now and six. Just let me know when you want the next one. Two for one on pizza, too, but you'd better order soon if you want one."

The place wasn't crowded, but it started filling up fast. "Can I get a small one?"

"Sure, what do you want on it?"

"You got pepperoni and black olives?"

69

"No problem. I'll put that right in."

Tim was still working on his first beer and waiting for his pizza when St. John walked in. He paused for a second, looked around, and made his way to an empty table directly across from where Tim was sitting. *Well, well, well. This is interesting,* Tim thought. He was so involved with watching St. John that he never noticed when his pizza came.

"Here you go, pal," the bartender told him, and went to take care of another customer.

Careful, Tim told himself when he realized he had been staring. *I don't want him to notice me.* When he turned back to his pizza, he realized he could watch St. John in the mirror that filled the wall behind the bar. He almost choked on his beer when two more of the guys he had seen outside Celeste's tent joined him at the table. A minute later one more walked in and sat down with them. That only left Paul Bunyan. Tim couldn't help but wonder if the big man would show up, too.

A second after the last guy sat down, a waitress placed a pitcher and five glasses on their table. She was gone before any of them could say anything. Tim was surprised when they all looked at the pitcher, but none of them reached for it. A minute later, the buzz in the bar quieted and all four of the men looked toward the door. Tim glanced that way in the mirror and saw the big man come in. It was the first time he had seen him since that day at the fair. *Damn, he looked big on the Midway, but here, inside this bar, he looks huge.*

Tim watched the giant walk over to the table where the other four sat. He stopped when he saw the pitcher of beer on the table. Tim could see the frown on his face and hear him ask, "Who ordered the beer?"

The men at the table all looked at each other as if no one wanted to claim that they had. Then one of them, not St. John, answered. "No one. Missy just brought it over on her own."

Miller didn't look happy about it. "Missy did, did she? Well, okay then," he answered in a voice loud enough for the entire bar to hear. Then he sat down, filled his glass, and placed the pitcher back on the table. That seemed to be the signal the others needed to fill their glasses. Before any of them could even take a sip from their beers, Stu drained his glass and poured himself a second. "Drink up, boys. We need our second pitcher. Each man did as he was told and quickly finished their drinks. The second round went down almost as fast as the first. Miller then emptied what was left into his glass, turned, and called to the waitress, "Missy, another pitcher over here." The waitress gave him a resigned look and went to the bar to fetch it.

After pouring the pitcher for Missy, the bartender drew a second glass for Tim. "What's that all about," Tim asked, nodding at the mirror.

"Just watch, you'll see."

Miller grinned at the waitress as she approached the table with the full pitcher. The way he had positioned himself, the woman had no choice but to reach past him to place it on the table. As soon as she did, she tried to quickly back away. It didn't do any good. Miller reached out and grabbed her ass before she could step out of his reach.

"He always do that?" Tim asked.

"Every time."

"Why doesn't somebody say something?"

"Look at him. Why don't you say something?"

"Not me. I'm new here."

Tim nursed his beer and ate his pizza, all the while splitting his attention between the television over the bar and the men at the table.

"We owe you another pizza, if you want it," the bartender told him when he took Tim's empty pan away.

Tim really didn't, but he wasn't ready to leave yet. "Sure, why not. I can always take what I don't eat home, right?"

"Right. You want another beer?

"No thanks. I have to walk home."

The bartender laughed. "Hah. Those guys will go through at least two more pitchers and they're all driving."

He was right. Miller and his friends had no problem having another beer. Before the two-for-one happy hour was over, they had gone through two large pizzas and five pitchers of beer and still had another free one coming. Every time the waitress came near their table, Miller grabbed her ass and laughed. Each time he did, his crew of bootlickers laughed right along with him.

"Those guys are getting hammered. Do they do this every week or just on two-for-one night?"

"Just two-for-one night. They all come in once in a while, have a beer or two and leave, but they're here as a group every one of these nights."

"They always get hammered like this?"

"This? This is nothing. They'll be here another two hours and drink at least two more pitchers. I'm waiting for one of them to kill themselves, or someone else, when they drive home."

"They ever get stopped for DUI?"

"Of course not. The sheriff is Cole Miller, the big

guy's brother."

"Too bad," Tim said, but he was already thinking about the next two-for-one night.

* * *

Bucky St. John was feeling it when he noticed the guy at the bar watching them in the mirror. He thought of mentioning it to Stu, but his glass was empty and the pitcher was coming around. He took it and had to concentrate on not spilling any. He managed it, and when he looked back up, the guy was gone. *Must have been my imagination.*

If he had been here by himself, or with just one of the other guys, Bucky would have left before he got so shitfaced. But when he was with Stu, he didn't dare leave before the big guy, none of them did, and no one passed on another beer until Stu had decided they had had enough. So, like it or not, he was stuck here for another couple of hours and would have one hell of a hangover in the morning.

God, I'm drunk, he thought when he finally stepped outside. After the warmth of the bar, the cold night air hit him like a slap in the face. He took several deep breaths to try and clear his head before getting into his car. Once inside, he opened the door and rolled down the driver's side window.

St. John made the drive home creeping along at a mere ten miles an hour with the window open and the radio blasting. He was drunk, but he wasn't stupid. If he lost it and went off the road at ten miles an hour, at least he wouldn't kill himself. The dog started barking when he pulled into his trailer, but stopped when he got out and yelled at it. "Stupid fucking dog, you can sleep out here tonight. I'll teach you to bark at me."

It took four tries to get the key into the lock on the trailer door. Once he was inside, he collapsed on the bed without bothering to get undressed.

Chapter Twelve

Celeste spread the cards in front of her on the table. One of her attackers was gone. That left five. She had dreamed of Tim every night since leaving him in Barkham. Sometimes he was there with her. He constantly filled her thoughts. They had only spent two days together, but she ached for him. She knew he was the other half of her being. But she had waited fifty years for him in a different life. Had she found happiness in that life, or had it been filled with bitterness and regret? She would never know. That life was meaningless now. It had filled its purpose by sending Tim to her. How soon until Tim eliminated another one of them?

Chapter Thirteen

Something in the way Tim looked or acted must have told Estella that he had gone to Kelly's and had a good time. "I told you all you needed was to get out and have some fun."

"Yeah, you were right. It was good. I had a few beers, a pizza, two actually, and figured some things out."

"Oh, no. You're not leaving are you?"

"What? No. I'm happy here. I just had a few things I had to work out."

"Did you meet anyone? A girl, maybe?"

"No," Tim laughed. He almost said, "I have a girl," but didn't want to have to explain that.

Estella gave him a queer look that puzzled him. Then he got it. "Yes, I like girls. I'm just looking for the right one. I'll know her when I find her."

When she gave him an embarrassed smile, Tim quickly changed the subject. "I've never been in Vermont during the winter. How cold does it get up here?"

"Pretty darn cold, and we get a lot of snow. You're going to need a parka, gloves, boots, and a good warm hat. I'd go to Sampson's Ski Shop for those."

"I can't get them here?"

"You can, but Sampson's is the place to get a really warm jacket."

"Yeah, but I don't get a ten percent discount at Sampson's."

"Oh," Estella answered, embarrassed again.

* * *

Tim spent the next four weeks anticipating what he was going to do with St. John. Eliminating the man would be easy. Making him suffer, and making sure he knew why, was going to be the hard part.

On the third Thursday of October, Tim dressed entirely in black and waited until it was dark to walk to Kelly's. It was chilly enough that his breath fogged as he walked and he was glad he had worn a sweatshirt under his windbreaker. Along the way, he made sure to duck out of sight of any headlights that would have revealed his presence. He had no intention of anyone remembering a man walking alone on the road that night.

The parking lot was full when Tim got to Kelly's. St. John's Buick was in the second row. He stood in the shadows until he was sure no one was outside. Then he walked over to the Buick and tried the door handle. As he had expected, it was unlocked. That would have never happened in 2006. The interior light popped on when he opened the door, but there was no help for that. He was inside with the door closed and the light off within a matter of seconds. Now all he had to do was wait.

Huddling in the back of St. John's car brought back memories of the nights he had spent in Nam. Memories he had buried deep bubbled to the surface of his mind. Instead of forcing them back to where they had been hidden, he embraced them, letting them establish the mindset he needed to be in for what he was about to do.

Tim had no idea how long he had been waiting when the driver's side door opened and the interior lights flashed on. All he knew was that it was long enough for St. John to get good and drunk. He could hear the man mumbling to himself as he started the car. When they were moving, a cold wind whistled through the vehicle and Tim knew St. John must have left the window open. He was starting to have second thoughts about his plan; this idiot could kill them both before he went a mile.

As soon as Tim felt the car slow to a stop, he sat up and put a knife to St. John's throat. "Pull it over and put it in park."

"What?" St. John slurred.

"Pull over and put it in park or you're a dead man."

St. John started to argue, but a prick with the tip of the knife convinced him to do as he was told.

"What do you want? You want money? I've only got about twenty bucks, but you can have it."

"This isn't about money. It's about the woman you and your buddies raped."

Tim felt St. John stiffen. In the rearview mirror, he saw the fear come into the man's eyes.

"What woman? We didn't rape no woman."

"Oh, but you did. She told me all about it — how

you took her from her trailer, carried her out to the woods, and then took turns raping her."

"It was Stu. After he was done with her, he said we all had to do her. I didn't want to, but I had to."

Tim knew that was a lie from his dream. Bucky had been just as anxious as the rest to have his turn at Celeste. He was about to say, "Bull shit," when the unmistakable smell of urine filled the car. "Bucky, did you just piss yourself? A big, bad rapist like you? What would Stu say if he knew you pissed yourself?"

St. John didn't answer.

"Were you first after Miller, or were you later? Did you cheer the others on? How about when Baker pulled her head back and hit her? Did you laugh like you do when Stu grabs that waitress's ass?" He knew the answers to all these questions, but he wanted St. John to think about what he'd done and why he was going to die.

All the time he was talking, he kept eye contact with St. John in the mirror. When the man started crying and begging for his life, Tim decided it was enough. He grabbed St. John's head and snapped his neck. Asshole number two was gone, but his work wasn't finished. Now he had to make it look like an accident. He didn't want to spook the rest of them. Not yet at least.

Tim scrambled into the front seat, made sure the emergency brake was off, and propped St. John's right foot on the accelerator. The dead weight pushed the pedal to the floor. The motor revved with the roar of a V8. Tim got out the passenger's side door and walked around to the driver's side. As he reached across St. John to drop the shift lever into D, he thought of another slogan from his past life — "Friends should never let friends drive drunk." Good advice, but it wasn't going to help St. John.

Tim had to jump back when the Buick took off with a chirp from the rear tires. He watched the tail lights shrink in the night, waiting for them to veer off the road. For a while, it seemed like they never would. *Come on, come on, before a car comes the other way.* He breathed a sigh of relief when he saw the lights veer into the woods and bounce into the air when the Buick hit a tree. A second later, the sound of the crash reached him.

* * *

Celeste was in South Carolina when the sudden flash ran through her body telling her Tim had burned one of the tarot cards. Another of her assailants was dead. The shadow in her mind got a little less dark. Tonight, when they met in their dreams, she would see exactly what Tim had done. Then she would dream of the rape, and there would only be four men when she did.

Chapter Fourteen

Sheriff Miller received the call from the deputy on duty a little after midnight. "Cole, you might want to come out to the Barkham–Tolland Road. We've had a fatal accident out here."

"Shit, how many?"

"Just one. It's Bucky St. John. Looks like he was coming home drunk from Kelly's and lost control of his car. He ran it off the road and into a tree."

Miller swore again. He had known this was going to happen one day. He'd told Stu and his buddies to cool it, but Stu had laughed in his face, and so had the rest of them. "Don't worry, we're all big boys," his brother had said. Well, now one of those big boys was dead. That made two of Stu's posse in two months. It had just been bad luck for Hubie, but it was bad judgment for St. John. Maybe this would drill a little sense into the others. He doubted it, but he could hope.

Cole saw the red lights of the car on the scene

flashing from a mile away. Ted Swanson had set out flares and was directing traffic around the crash site. "You call for an ambulance yet?" Cole asked through his window when he pulled up.

"Yeah, but it's not going to do St. John any good. The steering wheel crushed his chest."

Cole parked his cruiser and went to look at St. John's car. It was a mess. The Buick had hit a big maple tree. Its front end was wrapped around the trunk. *He must have been moving when he lost it. The damn trunk is two feet into the engine compartment.*

When he looked inside, he could see Swanson was right. The steering column had pushed back into St. John and pinned him against the back seat, crushing his chest. From the way his neck was bent, it looked like that had been broken, too.

I guess I'd better tell Stu in the morning. Sawyer Gaunt said he was pretty pissed about being the last one to hear about Hubie Martin.

The ambulance arrived ten minutes after Cole. After one look inside the car, Glenn Bisham, the driver, just shook his head. "Better call the Fire Department, Sheriff. We're never going to be able to get him out of there."

Cole was about to ask Swanson if he had called them when he heard the blare of a siren and saw the fire truck's lights flashing in the dark. They arrived at the scene a minute later. Chief John Geldart walked over to the car, took one look at it, and the body inside, and came back to Miller. "We're going to have to haul that out of there before we can get the body out."

"Okay, do it."

Geldart and the other men on the truck hitched the winch to the back bumper of the Buick and pulled it away from the tree and onto the road. Pieces of the front bumper and grille dropped onto the ground when the car separated from the tree. Once they had the Buick on the road, Geldart had them work on freeing St. John from the front seat. He was wedged so tight between the steering wheel and the seat that they had to remove the back of it to get him out. When they had him free, they placed him on a stretcher and carried him to the waiting ambulance.

Swanson walked over as the fire truck was pulling out. "I called for a tow, but they can't get here 'til morning. What do you want to do?"

Miller wasn't surprised. Chick Kerwin wasn't the kind that would crawl out of a warm bed on a cold night to tow a wreck back to town. He could get away with it because he was the only show in town since Hubie Martin had died.

"Fine, put some new flares out and stay out here with it. I'll send Chris out when he comes in."

Miller could tell Swanson wasn't thrilled with the idea, but he didn't care. It was Swanson's shift after all. Cole had already been here for three hours, and he needed to get at least a couple hours of sleep before he took on the task of notifying Eric St. John that his brother was dead.

* * *

Cole groaned and rolled over when the alarm went off at six. He wanted to shut it off and go back to sleep, but he couldn't. He had to see Eric St. John before the man left for work. Then he'd go see Stu. He was showered, shaved, and dressed in twenty minutes. Fifteen minutes after that, he was knocking on Eric St.

John's door.

Carol St. John answered the knock at the door in her robe. "What's Bucky done now?" she asked as soon as she saw Cole.

"Is Eric here?" Cole asked.

"I'll get him," Carol sighed.

When Eric came to the door, he had the same question as Carol. "What's he done now?"

Cole steeled himself, then just came out with it. "Bucky's dead. He was killed in an accident last night."

Eric's response was not what Cole had expected. "He was drunk, right?"

"Right," Cole answered. "He was coming back from Kelly's. He went off the road and hit a tree."

"Well, it was bound to happen sooner or later. Did he kill anybody else?"

"No," Cole answered. "It was a single-car accident."

"Okay, thanks for letting me know," St. John told him and started to close the door.

"Wait, what do you want me to do with his body?"

"I don't care. Do anything you want with it. He stopped being my brother a long time ago," St. John replied, and shut the door.

Jesus, that didn't go well. I wonder what happened between those two. Stu may be an asshole, but I still love him.

* * *

Stu heard the pounding on the door, rolled over, and saw that it was 9:30. *What idiot is pounding on my door at this time of the morning? This had better be good, or I'm going to kick some ass.*

When he opened the door wearing nothing but boxers, Stu was ready to raise hell with whoever was out there. "What the hell do you …" He stopped when he saw it was his brother. "What happened?"

"Bucky St. John drove his car off the road last night. He's dead."

"Fuck. Come on in and tell me about it."

Stu led him to the kitchen. "So, what happened?" he asked while he was putting a pot of coffee on the stove.

"Well, I figure he was drunk as a skunk. You were all at Kelly's last night, right?"

"Yeah," Stu admitted.

"I warned you guys this was going to happen someday. At least he didn't kill anyone else. It was a single-car accident. He drove that Buick right into a big maple tree. He had to be going at least sixty."

Stu gave his brother a look of disbelief. "Asshole. He always told us he never went over twenty on his way home."

"Well, he wasn't doing twenty last night. Okay, I've told you what I had to, now I have to get back to work."

"Hey," Stu called to his brother, "what's going to happen to that dog of his?"

"I don't know. I hear he's a mean bastard. You want him?"

"Maybe. I'll go over and take a look at him."

"Fine, you do that. I can have somebody take him to the pound if you don't want him. Just let me know."

* * *

After leaving his brother's, Cole drove to Kelly's to talk to Pete Conway. "So, how drunk did the boys get last night?" he asked the bartender.

"They were wasted. They do this every two-for-one night. I'm surprised this didn't happen sooner. I always said one of them was going to kill themselves on their way home."

"If they get that drunk, why don't you cut them off?"

Conway shook his head at the stupidity of the question. "Cut them off? Right. I tried that once and Stu threatened to bust me and the bar up. Now I just let them get as wasted as they want and hope they leave without any trouble."

"If it's that bad, why didn't you call me?"

Conway shot him a look of disbelief. "Like that would help."

* * *

Stu had no intention of taking the damn dog. Cole was right; it was one mean son of a bitch. If it were up to him, he'd just shoot the fucker and save the town some trouble. But the mutt was a good excuse to go over to Bucky's trailer. There might be some shit over there he could use.

The dog started barking as soon as Stu pulled into the drive. He parked far enough away from the beast so it couldn't reach him when he got out of his truck. The thing went wild, barking and snapping at him when he went to the trailer. Stu ignored it.

He was afraid he was going to have to break in, but when he tried the door, it was unlocked.

Idiot, he thought, and then remembered Bucky laughing about how he almost locked himself out because he couldn't get his key in the lock the last time he got plastered. Once he was inside, Stu went through the trailer with practiced ease. He found fifty-three bucks in a dresser drawer, a .22 target pistol and a box of shells in a bedside stand, and a bottle of rum in the kitchen cabinet over the sink. Nothing else interested him. He was in and out in less than fifteen minutes. As soon as he stepped out of the door, the damn dog strained at its chain and started barking and growling at him. *Fuck you, dog. You can starve out here for all I care.*

Chapter Fifteen

Sheriff Cole Miller had a body … and a problem. Actually, the body was the problem. Eric St. John had refused to have anything to do with Bucky, and no one had come forward to claim his body. George Wills wouldn't bury him without being paid. The town, or the state, was going to have to foot the bill for his burial. If they waited for the state, St. John wouldn't be in the ground until next spring. "Go ahead and bury him. Send the bill to the Town Hall. And keep it cheap," he told Wills.

"You want a viewing?"

"Sure. We should at least do that for him. One day, then plant him."

After he left Wills', Cole drove back to his brother's place to tell him about the viewing and the funeral. When he pulled into Stu's driveway, his truck was gone, so Cole left him a note. "Viewing for St. John at Wills' Funeral Home tomorrow night at six. Funeral the next day at ten." Cole doubted his brother would go, but he had told him. The rest was up to Stu.

Funny, Cole thought as he drove back to town, *Hubie Martin and Bucky St. John, two of Stu's buddies killed in two months. They've been hanging around Stu since high school. Bad luck.*

There was no need for Cole to tell Gaunt, Burke, or Baker about St. John. By now the news would be all over town. Cole would stop in at the viewing, of course; St. John had been three years behind him in high school, and he had seen him at the house whenever he was there with Stu. He'd go in uniform so the town would be represented, too.

* * *

Sawyer, Bill, and Jack stood together at the back of the viewing room in Wills' Funeral Home. None of them were surprised that they were the only ones there. Sheriff Miller was the only other person to even stop in. They had each hoped Stu might show up, but none of them actually thought he would. By the way they fidgeted, it was obvious none of them wanted to be there. What none of them would say, but they all knew, was that they didn't dare leave. If they did and Stu showed up after they were gone, there'd be hell to pay. They left together when the viewing ended at eight.

"How about we head over to Kelly's and drink a pitcher for Bucky?" Jack Baker suggested when they were outside. Sawyer and Jack looked at each other, then nodded. "Okay, then. Let's go."

When they walked into Kelly's, their usual table was already taken, so they sat at another. Missy stopped by a minute later. "You boys here alone tonight, or is your glorious leader coming, too?"

"It's just us," Baker answered.

"Sorry about your friend," she told them, but she didn't sound all that sincere. "You guys want a beer?"

"We'll take a pitcher," Baker told her.

"This is it. One pitcher," Missy told them when she set in on the table. "We don't need anyone else getting killed." It wasn't lost on any of them that was the first time Missy had stayed around their table long enough to do anything other than take their order or drop something off.

Baker poured for all of them and then raised his glass. "To Bucky."

"To Bucky," Burke and Gaunt echoed.

They sat and nursed the pitcher, reminiscing about things they had done together with, and without, Stu. None of them mentioned last summer's rape.

"Either of you guys going to the burial tomorrow?" Baker asked as they were getting ready to leave.

"I don't think so," Gaunt answered.

"Me either," chimed in Burke. "How about you?"

"Not if you guys aren't going. We said our good-byes tonight."

* * *

While Baker, Burke, and Gaunt were sitting in Kelly's, Tim was determining which of them would be the next to die by drawing a name out of his hat. *Who's next*, he wondered as he withdrew a folded slip of paper. It was Gaunt. He then drew one of the three remaining tarot cards — a blindfolded figure holding a sword and a set of scales — Judgment.

Judgment. Tim didn't know what the card might

mean to an adept, but he knew what it meant for Sawyer Gaunt. A quote from *A Knight's Tale*, a movie he had seen, explained it perfectly: *You have been weighed, you have been measured, and you definitely have been found wanting.* In Gaunt's case, they were words to die by. Not too soon, though. If he moved too soon, it would become apparent someone was targeting Miller's crew.

Chapter Sixteen

Halloween came and Tim was once again reminded of the differences between the world he was
living in now and the one he had left behind. Kids
wandered the streets in homemade costumes. There
wasn't a store-bought one to be seen. Only the little
ones had parents trailing along behind them. Any kid
eight or up was either alone or with a small group of
friends. High school kids had painted store windows
with Halloween scenes that were judged by the school
art teacher and voted on by the citizens of Barkham.
Prizes were given out to the top three. Since Tim
lived on the third floor, there would be no knocks on
his door, so he sat outside on a bench and watched
the ghosts, witches, and princesses parade by.

A week later, the cold hit Vermont like a hammer.
Tim woke up to frost-covered windows and clanking
steam pipes. His room was too cold if he opened a
window and too warm if he left it closed. The water

in the shower took several minutes to get hot as it traveled from the heater in the basement to his third-floor apartment. When he stepped outside, he hustled across the thirty feet from his alcove to Woolworth's front door. He had to stand there blowing warm air into his hands and thanking God he had put out the extra money for a good parka as he waited for Meek to unlock the door and let him in. The first thing he did was get a warm pair of gloves and a hat from the men's department and put them at the register. He'd pay for them later. He didn't want to risk someone else buying them before he got off work.

When Estella arrived at five to nine, he was waiting to let her in so she wouldn't have to stand outside in the cold. When she hustled through the door, the frigid air followed her. It was going to be like that the whole day. "Oh, thank you. It's freezing out there," she told him as she shucked her parka. She wore a sweater underneath her coat that she'd wear all day to keep the chill off as cold air rushed in each time a customer came in or left.

As the days shortened and nightfall came earlier each day, Tim felt the walls of the apartment closing in on him. It made him realize how much he had become accustomed to the mental distractions television, movies, and the internet provided. Books and the radio could fill some of the hours, but he needed something else. On his next day off, he was going was going to look for a television. Maybe he could find one second-hand. He'd ask Estella; she might know where he could get one.

* * *

"Stell, do you know any place I can pick up a used T.V.?" he asked her at work the next day.

Estella thought for a minute, then nodded. "Try Burke's T.V. and Appliances. It's on Elm, just off Main Street."

"Great, I'll check it out on Sunday."

"I think he's closed on Sunday. I know he's open on Monday, though."

"Okay, thanks. I'll go over on Monday."

* * *

Tim walked into Burke's T.V. and Appliances early Monday morning. The front of the store was filled with new televisions and appliances. These were out of his league, plus he couldn't imagine carrying any of them up two flights of stairs. Still, it didn't hurt to look, or reminisce. He remembered T.V.s like these in his parent's house back in the day. An RCA console model with a 21" screen on one side and a radio on the other looked really familiar. He looked, and sure enough, a turntable was hidden behind the radio under a lift-up lid. The top of this one was bare. The one in his parent's house had had a ceramic tiger fighting a python perched on it. It was god-awful ugly and his mother hated it, but his father insisted on keeping it. Tim couldn't remember what had happened to the thing. One day it had just disappeared.

"Can I help you?" a male voice asked, jerking him out of his memories.

Tim answered without turning around. He was still wrapped up in these relics from his youth. "I'm looking for a T.V., something cheap, maybe a used one if you have anything like that?"

"I do. I have a few I took in trade in the back. Would you like to see them?"

"That'd be great," Tim answered and turned a-round to follow the man to the back of the store. He froze when he saw the man's face. Then it clicked — Burke's T.V. Burke was one of the names Martin had given him. This was another of the bastards who had been with Miller at the fair, one of the bastards who had raped Celeste. He recovered in time and the man did not pick up on his surprise.

"Here are three you might be interested in," Burke said when they reached the back of the store.

Tim looked them over and picked a 10" portable that had a thin layer of dust covering it. "How much for this one?"

Burke reached past Tim and looked at a white tag tied to the antenna. "It's marked twenty, but it's been here for a while. You can have it for ten."

"Seems fair. I'll take it if it works."

Burke picked it up and carried it to a work bench, where he plugged it in. "I'm sure it does, but let's check it out." When he turned the set on, a bright white dot appeared in the middle of the screen. It quickly ex-panded into a static-filled black-and-white picture. "It gets better if you adjust the antenna," he told him. Sure enough, it did get better when he extended the antenna to its full length. "That's okay, but you might want some rabbit ears, too. That way you'll be able to get all the stations." He demonstrated by changing the channel; the picture changed from sharp back to fuzzy. "I'll hook up a set of rabbit ears so you can see the difference."

Tim stared daggers at Burke's back as he went to get the rabbit ears. He would have liked nothing more than to whack the bastard right here, right now, but he couldn't. Someday, though.

When the rabbit ears worked as promised, Tim said he'd take those, too. It turned out they were almost as expensive as the T.V.

"Used televisions don't come with a warranty. What you see is what you get. I just want to make sure you know that before you take it."

"That's fine," Tim agreed.

"The best reception is with a roof-mounted antenna. I have those, too, if you can use one."

"This will be fine. I don't have anywhere for a roof antenna."

Tim left, carrying the television by the handle on the top with his right hand and the rabbit ears in his left. He was extremely pleased with his outing. Not only did he get the television he wanted, but he found one of the men he was looking for. Burke's day would come, but Gaunt was still next.

That night, when darkness fell, Tim had an electronic buddy to keep him company. There were only three channels instead of the hundred or so he was used to, but that was three more than he had had the night before. Soon, he'd be spending his evenings with the likes of Ed Sullivan, James Arness, and Alfred Hitchcock. He only wished *Star Trek* had been around in 1956. It wouldn't make its debut until 1966. He had missed a lot of the early years when he was in Nam.

* * *

November came and went and still Tim didn't feel the time was right to deal with Gaunt. Then, two days before Christmas, as he stood freezing his ass off in front of the town Christmas tree with all its lights, he knew that Gaunt's time had finally come. Sawyer Gaunt was going to die on New Year's Eve. He would be the first, but not last, fatality of 1957. Tim could guarantee there would be at least three more after him.

On Sunday, December 30th, Tim took his mind off Gaunt by spending the afternoon in front of his television watching the NFL Championship game between the New York Giants and the Chicago Bears with a pizza from Antonio's and six pack of Bud. For the life of him, he couldn't remember who had won. Thinking back, he realized he hadn't been much of a football fan in those days. Apparently, neither was the rest of the country. There was none of the hype he was used to surrounding the Super Bowl. Names that were now a part of history kept popping up throughout the broadcast: Frank Gifford, Rosie Brown, Sam Huff, Andy Robustelli, Vince Lombardi, and Tom Landry.

The Bears came into the game as slight favorites, but ended up losing 47 to 7. The game was played at Yankee Stadium, where the temperature was twenty degrees Fahrenheit. Both teams were from cold weather cities, but the Giant's elected to wear sneakers instead of cleats. The tactic worked because they had much better footing on the frozen field than the Bears.

Tim had been back to Kelly's Pub twice since he had been there in September, but never on a two-for-one night when he knew Miller and his boys would be there. On those nights he had waited outside so when Miller and his crew left, he'd be able to identify which vehicle belonged to whom. Gaunt drove a 4-door, 1952 Chevy Belair; Baker drove a 2-door, 1950 Hudson; and

Burke got behind the wheel of a beat-up 1947 Ford Custom. Miller drove a Ford F150 pickup. He had watched all of them leave Kelly's drunk after a night of drinking. None of them locked their cars. He was counting on Gaunt not locking his on New Year's Eve. Climbing into the back seat had worked so well with St. John that he'd decided to use the same strategy with Gaunt.

Tim waited until eleven before heading over to Kelly's. It was cold as hell, with two inches of new snow on the ground. He had no intention of getting there early and freezing his ass off for hours in the back of Gaunt's Chevy. The last thing he wanted to do was freeze to death while he waited for the man.

Tim almost panicked when he couldn't find Gaunt's car in Kelly's parking lot. He was ready to go home and curse his luck when he finally found it at the rear of the lot. He had just settled into the back seat when it started snowing. By the time Gaunt staggered out of the pub at 2:00 am, three more inches had piled up on the Chevy.

A shower of snow blew into the car when Gaunt opened his door. Tim could hear him cursing as he dug around the front seat for something. Then he must have realized what it was, the brush that was sitting on the back seat. "Fuck," Tim swore under his breath when the front door slammed shut. A second later another shower of snow erupted into the car when Gaunt opened the back door near Tim's head.

Gaunt reached in to grab the brush, and his eyes widened in surprise when he saw Tim. "Who the fuck are you, and what the hell are you doing in my car?" Tim grabbed him and dragged him into the back seat before he could step back.

Gaunt was strong, but he was drunk. Tim was able to push him onto the back seat and put him in a choke hold before he could fight back. Once Gaunt stopped struggling, Tim reached over and closed the back door. This was not going the way he had planned, but it was too late to back out now. With a little luck, he could still make this work. The snow that had just screwed him was going to help him now by preventing anyone from seeing inside the car.

Tim went through Gaunt's pockets looking for his car keys. He finally found them in the parka. Once he had them, he got out, cleared off just enough snow to allow him to drive, started the car, and drove out of Kelly's parking lot. Now he just had to make it through town and onto the road to Gaunt's.

What should have been a ten-minute drive took over twenty-five due to the snow. As soon as he was off the main road, Tim stopped the car, dragged Gaunt out of the back seat, dropped him on the side of the road and drove the Chevy into a ditch. By the time he was done, Gaunt was starting to come around. *Good, I've got things I need to tell him,* Tim thought.

"Gaunt, you awake? Can you hear me?"

"Yeah, who the hell are you? What are you doing?" Gaunt mumbled, trying to comprehend what was happening to him.

"I'm Judgment."

"What the hell does that mean?"

"It means you've been weighed, you've been measured, and you've definitely been found wanting."

"What the hell does *that* mean?" Gaunt mumbled

"It means you're going to die."

"What? Why?"

"Because you raped a woman at the fair."

Gaunt tried to push Tim away, but he was still drunk. Then a light must have gone off in his head. "You killed Hubie and Bucky, didn't you?" Then he started to cry. "Don't, don't. I'm sorry. I don't want to die."

"Too late for that," Tim told him, and choked him into unconsciousness again. Then he opened Gaunt's parka and rolled him down the embankment. As drunk as he was, and as cold as it was, Gaunt wouldn't last a half hour.

The walk back to his apartment was a trial he wouldn't have been able to make back in July. When he finally arrived there, he was close to exhaustion. After climbing the stairs to his apartment on the third floor, he took a hot shower and collapsed into bed. In the morning he would burn the card.

* * *

Celeste was in Sarasota, Florida, when she had the dream of Gaunt's demise. She wouldn't feel the burn from the tarot card until the morning. In her dream tonight there would only be two men in line behind the big man.

* * *

Chet Stewart found Gaunt's car at two that afternoon. He had been plowing since the storm had started, but most of that time was spent trying to keep the main roads open. He stopped the plow and climbed down the embankment to make sure no one was in it. When he found it unoccupied, he called it in and kept on plowing.

As soon as things started to calm down around the station, Cole sent Chris Chambliss out to check on the car Stewart had called about. Chris found it without any trouble, but he had to scramble over a mountain of plowed snow to reach it. He cleared the windows enough to peer inside and verify no one was in it. When he saw it was empty, he made his way back to his cruiser and notified Cole.

When the car was still there on Monday, Cole sent Chambliss back to check the registration to see who it belonged to. When Chambliss called back, he sounded out of breath from climbing back to his cruiser. "Cole, Chris here. The car belongs to Sawyer Gaunt. He's one of your brother's friends, isn't he?"

"Yeah," Cole answered, and a chill ran up his spine that had nothing to do with the weather.

The first call Cole made was to Gaunt's number. After twelve rings he gave up. The next call he made was to his brother. Stu answered on the fourth ring. "When's the last time you saw Sawyer Gaunt," he asked when Stu came on the line.

"New Year's Eve, why?"

"Because his car's been sitting in a snowbank since the storm. We checked, but it's empty. I've called his house and no one answers. You have any idea where he might be if he wasn't there?"

"Did you try Burke or Baker? He might be with one of them."

"No, but I'll try them next. I'll get back to you if I locate him."

Cole's next call went to Baker. He hadn't seen or heard from Gaunt either. He got the same results from Burke. Now he was sure something was wrong.

Cole, Chambliss, and Swanson gathered at the

spot where Gaunt's Chevy had gone off the road. Each of them had a long, thin metal pole. "Start here and work out," Cole told them. Each man started poking his pole into the snow looking for a body. Chambliss found it five feet from the Chevy. "Over here," he called as he brushed snow away from Gaunt.

"Ah, shit," Miller said when he saw the corpse. "You guys brush the snow off him, and I'll call an ambulance to come get him. Then you can head back to the office. I'll stay here with the body."

Miller sat in his car with the motor running and the heat on while he waited. *Assholes, all of them. I thought they might wise up after St. John had his accident. I guess that was too much to ask for.*

When the ambulance arrived, Glenn Bisham took one look at the body and told Miller they were going to need some help getting it out of the ditch. "Why? Just go down there and get him," Cole demanded.

"That's not going to happen," the driver told him. "He's frozen solid and the snow's too deep. We'll tie him to a stretcher and then we can pull it out with a rope. It's going to take all three of us for that."

"Fine, let's do it," Miller agreed.

As Cole watched the attendants struggle to get the frozen body on to the stretcher, all he could think of was that it was like moving one of the green plastic soldiers he had played with as a kid. Once they had the body on, the driver climbed out of the ditch and handed Cole the rope. "We'll pull from up here and Dave will try to keep it from digging into the snow." Even with three of them working together it took them ten minutes to get the body up and on to the road.

Thank God he's not married. At least I don't have to do that again, Cole thought as he watched the ambulance head back to town with the body.

Chapter Seventeen

Tim placed the two remaining slips of paper with the names written on them on the table. Then he covered each with a tarot card — Death on the right, The Moon on the left. Which one to pick? That was the question. Not wanting to make the decision himself, he dug into his pocket and pulled out a quarter. *Heads it's Death, tails, the Moon*

Tim flipped the quarter and watched it tumble in the air. When it hit the table, it bounced once and came to a stop tails up. The decision had been made — The Moon.

"Who are you, Mister Moon?" he asked the slip of paper before he unfolded it to reveal the name. It turned out to be Jack Baker. He didn't have to look under the other card to know that Bill Burke was Death.

* * *

Three of Stu's crew dead in just over five months. They all looked like accidents, but three? Two could have been a coincidence. Three was pushing it. Cole suspected someone out there was settling an old score. The problem was, there were a lot of old scores out there to settle.

I need to talk to my brother to see if he has any ideas about who it might be.

* * *

Stu looked at Cole and just shook his head. "That's crazy. You actually think someone is going after my guys?"

"I do. Two of your crew dying could have been a coincidence. Three of them getting killed in five months isn't. Something's going on, and I don't like it."

"They were all accidents. Two of them because they were drunk. That's all it is."

"I don't think so, so humor me. Can you think of anyone who would do this? Anyone you really screwed over that I don't know about."

Stu thought about it. There were a few, that was for sure, but he couldn't tell Cole about those without really putting him on the spot. "No," he said with a straight face, but he knew his brother well enough to know he didn't believe him.

"Well, regardless, I'm going to stop and talk to Baker and Burke about it. If someone is out there killing your crew, I at least want them to be careful."

Stu knew it wouldn't do any good to argue about it with Cole, so he let it go. He'd talk to them, too.

As soon as Cole's cruiser was gone, Stu called

Burke and Baker to tell them to get their asses over to his place, pronto, but neither of them answered the phone. *Fuck, where the hell are you guys?*

He didn't have to wait long to find out. Baker called him within the hour. Cole must have talked to him at work.

"Jesus, Stu, Cole thinks somebody's out to get us. He thinks Hubie, Sawyer, and Bucky were murdered."

"Calm down, Jack. He was up here, too, and I told him it was all bullshit. Hubie got careless, and Sawyer and Bucky were drunk off their asses. I always tell you guys not to drive when you're shit-faced. Does anybody listen? No." Truth be told, he had never told them any such thing, but Jack would never have the balls to argue with him. "Call Bill. Tell him to meet us at my place tonight and we'll talk about it."

"What time?"

"Seven," Stu told him. That way he wouldn't have to provide them dinner. *Fuck,* he thought after he hung up. *I forgot to tell him to bring beer.*

* * *

The boys pulled up early in Burke's car. Stu watched from his front window as they climbed out of the Ford. It was cold as a bitch out there. He could see their breath freezing in front of their faces as they exhaled. A second after he lost sight of them, he heard a knock on the door. He looked at his watch — five minutes of seven. He had told Baker seven, not five of seven. He'd let them wait. When he said seven, he meant seven. They should know that.

When he finally opened the door, both men waited for Stu to invite them in. When he finally told them,

"Get in here, you're letting all the heat out," they rushed in to get out of the cold.

"I guess Cole came to you with his bullshit theory that someone's coming after you boys."

"You think it's bullshit?" Baker asked.

"Of course it's bullshit. What did we ever do that was so bad someone would want to kill us?"

Burke started to say something, but a scowl from Stu shut him down.

"Look, even though it *is* bullshit, maybe we should change things up a bit just in case. No more getting drunk at Kelly's on two-for-one night. We can still go, but we limit it to two pizzas and two pitchers. Then we leave. Keep an eye out for anybody who doesn't fit in. Let *me* know if you see anything like that and *I'll take care of it.*"

Both of them knew what that meant, and they knew better than to argue with him.

"So, now that that's settled, you guys want a beer, or do you have to get going?"

Burke caught the hint. "Nah, we'd better get going. It's colder than a well digger's ass out there and tomorrow's a work day."

* * *

"What do you think?" Baker asked once they were in Burke's car.

"I want to think it's all bullshit, but I don't know. Stu's pissed off an awful lot of people over the years, and we've been there for a lot of it."

"Yeah, but bad enough to come after *us*. Why not him?"

"Who's crazy enough to go after him?"

"Yeah, right."

They drove in silence for five miles before Baker spoke up. "Let's stop at Kelly's and talk this over. I'm still not sure it's all bullshit."

"Yeah, me either. Better safe than sorry, right?"

"Right."

* * *

Even though their usual table was open, Burke and Baker took a booth in the back so they could talk without being overheard.

"Sorry about your friend," Missy told them when she came over to take their order. Both Burke and Baker nodded their thanks, but didn't say anything. "So, what can I get you boys tonight?"

"Draft, a cheeseburger, and fries," Baker answered. "Same for me," Burke agreed.

"Stu coming in?"

"No, we're alone."

"Good," Missy answered. "You guys really ought to dump that asshole. You know that, right?"

When neither of them answered, she left to place their order and get their beers.

"You know, she's probably right," Baker said when she left.

"Yeah, but it might be too late. What do you think about Cole's theory?"

"I don't know. But Christ, what if he's right? Can you think of anyone who might do this?"

Burke started to answer but stopped when Missy brought their beers. When she left, he started a list of possibilities. "How about that guy in St. Johnsbury? Stu beat him so bad he put him in the hospital. Or that guy from Canada we ripped off. He lost a bundle. Or ..."

Baker stopped him. "I get the idea. But how do we cut ourselves off from Stu?"

"Yeah, that's the problem, isn't it?" Burke answered.

Chapter Eighteen

The Moon — two dogs howling at a full moon with a woman's face in it. Celeste — Baker. Baker — the Moon. Baker — the full moon. When was the next full moon? Tim had no idea, but he could find out at work. There was bound to be a calendar in the store that would tell him, and he could use one for the apartment.

Before he was leaving work for the day, Tim browsed the calendars for one that showed the stages of the moon. He found several. All he had to do was choose one.

Dogs? No. Horses? No. Cats? Hell no. Picturesque Vermont? I can live with that.

When he was back in his room, he looked for the dates of upcoming full moons. Wednesday, January 16? Too soon. Thursday, February 14? Valentine's Day? That could work. Friday, March 15? The Ides of March? Perfect! That would be two and a half months between

Baker and Gaunt, enough time to let things calm down if Stu and the boys were getting jumpy. God knows they should be by now. That would also leave him three and a half months for Burke and Miller. Plenty of time.

Snow. It seemed Tim had never seen so much snow. That and the short days were playing havoc with his efforts to stay in shape. If this was 2006, he could have joined a gym. There was nothing like that around here now.

When he got out of work at 4:30, it was already dark, but it was also too early to go back and sit in an empty apartment. He would go for walks, or sometimes he would head home to read, watch television, listen to the radio, or exercise in his room. Other times he would have dinner at Annie's just to get out of the apartment. On Sundays and Mondays, when he had the day off, it was impossible to run because of all the snow. He had to find something else to do, otherwise he would start to go soft. Maybe Stell would have some ideas.

He brought it up at lunch the next day as they sat in the break room. "Stell, I've got a problem. I can't run in this weather. I'm going nuts just sitting around the apartment. I need something to keep active. Have you got any ideas?"

"You ever think of skiing?"

"Skiing? No. Besides, I don't have skis, and even if I did, how would I get to a mountain?"

"Not mountain skiing, cross-country skiing. You can do that anywhere, and it's great exercise."

"Still impossible. No skis, no boots. I'd need boots, right?"

"I might be able to help you there. My son used

to ski before he joined the Navy. I've still got all his stuff at the house. You could use it if the boots fit."

"Really, you wouldn't mind?"

"Of course not. The stuff's just gathering dust at my house. I'll dig it all out and bring it in tomorrow. He's about your size, so they should be okay."

"You sure?"

"Of course I'm sure."

Estella was good on her word. "Come with me to my car after work and I'll give you all the skiing stuff. I'm parked right out front today," she told him when he unlocked the door for her.

"Okay, thanks," Tim answered, grateful for her generosity.

Estella got off an hour later than Tim did, but he was waiting for her when she came out of the store. "There you are," she said when she saw him. "Good, you can get the skis out of the car."

When Tim opened the door, the skis were on the passenger side and spanned the space from the back all the way to the front. He was amazed when he got them out of the car. They weren't like any skis he had ever seen before. They were a few inches longer than he was tall and were only about two inches wide.

After putting the skis inside the front door, he came back for the rest. Estella gave him a box that held the boots and bindings. When he had those, she handed him the poles. "There you go. That should do it. Do you know how to use these?"

He almost answered, "No, but I've seen it on the Olympics," before he caught himself. Instead, he said, "No, but I'll figure it out."

"Well, if you have any questions, just ask."

* * *

Tim spread the gear out in front of him on the floor of the apartment. The first things he reached for were the boots. He was pleasantly surprised to find they were a size 11 ½. He wore a size 11 wide, but these might do. When he slipped them on and tightened the laces, they were okay. Not perfect, but okay. Now all he had to do was figure out how to use the skis.

The first step was to attach the boots to the skis. Unlike normal skis, these boots only attached at the toe. It allowed the heel to leave the ski when the skier was "walking" in them. Once he had that figured out, he was ready to try them out in the snow. Luckily, he had watched the 2002 Winter Olympics in Salt Lake City, so he had some idea of what he was doing.

After two weekends of practice in the parking lot out back, which included much swearing and a few blisters, Tim finally felt comfortable enough to strike out on a cross-country excursion. After breakfast at Annie's, he laced up his boots, gathered his skis and poles, and headed out of town in the direction of the fair grounds. Within a quarter mile, the plowed roads and shoveled sidewalks of town gave way to open fields and the occasional farm house.

Before placing his boots into the bindings, Tim took a deep breath of the cold Vermont air and stared off into the distance, admiring what had been lost in the name of progress. The open, snow-covered field ran unobstructed all the way down to the Connecticut River. In the distance, the snow-covered mountains of New Hampshire rose into a cloudless blue sky. Here and there the black trunks and branches of leafless trees added sharp contrast to the gentle arcs and swells of the fields. In 2006, this view would be blocked by a McDonald's or Burger King; he couldn't remember which one stood on this spot. To his back, on the opposite side of the road, a strip mall with a CVS, a Dunkin Donuts, and a dry cleaners would replace the open field there. In his future life, he never thought of what had been, only what was. Beauty had been replaced by convenience one small step at a time until the only thing left was convenience.

Okay, down to the river and back. That should be a good first outing, he told himself. He fumbled along for the first twenty yards or so, but after that, he got into a rhythm and things went more smoothly. *This is easier than I thought it would be. Let's hope it's as good a workout as I thought it would be.* What he didn't realize, but would find out when he reached the river and started back, was that his path had been all downhill. The slope was gentle but continuous. The way back was going to be a bitch.

By the time Tim got back to the road, he had forgotten about the beauty that surrounded him. His heart was pumping and his calves were on fire. All he wanted to do was get back to his apartment and take a hot shower.

Chapter Nineteen

Even though the deaths of Hubie Martin, Bucky St. John, and Sawyer Gaunt all looked like accidents, Cole couldn't shake the feeling that there was something more going on. He'd been cleaning up after Stu since their parents had died in an automobile accident the year after Cole had graduated from high school. His brother was an asshole and Cole knew it, but blood was blood, and that's all there was to it. He also knew Stu and his boys had pissed off a lot of people and fucked over just as many. He was pretty sure the gypsy from the fair last year wasn't the only woman Stu had raped in his day. There were rumors of it even back in high school, but it was rare that anyone ever came forward to report it. The few times that they had, Cole had taken care of it.

I'm going to have to start asking around. See if anyone knows of someone with an ax to grind. St. John and Gaunt were drinking at Kelly's the nights they died. I'll start there.

Kelly's was half full when Cole stopped in. It was still early, but it was Friday. Before long, there wouldn't be an open booth or table to be had, so he took a seat at the bar. "What can I get you, Sheriff," Pete Conway asked.

"A draft and a menu. Better yet, what's the special tonight?"

"Yankee pot roast, mashed potatoes, and broccoli."

"Sounds good. I'll have that."

"Bud, Schaefer, or Piels for the draft?"

"Schaefer."

"Coming up," Pete said as he grabbed a glass and started to fill it from the tap.

Pete set the beer in front of Cole and was about to walk away when Cole stopped him. "Pete, were you here on New Year's Eve?"

"Yeah, why?"

"Just wondering. My brother and his friends were in, too. I guess they got pretty drunk. That right?"

Pete's smile disappeared and a note of caution crept into his voice. "Maybe, I'm not sure. I didn't serve them. Missy did. They didn't sit at the bar; they had a booth."

Cole wasn't surprised by the change in Pete's expression and attitude. "I'm not looking to blame anybody, Pete. I'm just trying to find out what happened that night."

The man relaxed a bit, but Cole could tell he still didn't want to talk. *Yeah, Stu has that effect on people.*

"You should ask Missy. She might be able to help you."

"Okay. Would you ask her to come over?"

Cole watched as Pete went and said something to Missy. She glanced at Cole, looked annoyed, and finally came over. "Pete says you want to talk to me about New Year's Eve."

"My brother and his friends were here. Did anything happen? Did Stu get in anyone's face?"

Missy studied him for a second before answering. "Your brother's an asshole. And so are his friends. But you already know that."

Cole was surprised to hear her speak so openly about his brother. "Did something happen that night?"

"Something happens every night Stu and his boys are here. They aren't bad when he's not here, but they're asshole little fanboys when he is."

"What happened that night?"

"The same thing that happens on every two-for-one night. They sit at that table right over there and order pizzas and pitchers. Every time I bring anything to their table, your brother grabs my ass, and all his buddies think it's the funniest thing they've ever seen. Some nights I go home with black and blues that last for days."

"I've never heard of this before."

"Of course you haven't. Everybody knows you cover up for him, so why would anyone tell you anything?"

"Then why are you telling me now?"

"Because you asked. And because I've had it. The next time he grabs my ass, I'm going to shove one of those pizzas down his throat."

"Don't do that. Not because of me, but because my brother *is* an asshole. He's an asshole who always gets even, with interest."

"Screw him, and screw you, too," Missy said before she walked off to wait on another customer.

Cole was ready to leave when his dinner came.

He considered just getting up and leaving, but that wouldn't look good, so he stayed and ate an excellent, but tasteless Yankee pot roast.

Chapter Twenty

At the end of January, red hearts filled with choco-lates arrived at the store. If this had been Walmart in 2006, they would have been on the shelf weeks ago. Valentine's Day hadn't meant much to Tim the last few years, but this year it did. As soon as he saw the first box, thoughts of Celeste filled most of his waking moments, as well as his dreams at night. It was a new sensation for him, but it confirmed that she was, in-deed, his destiny.

For the first fourteen days in February, Tim didn't dwell on Baker or Burke. Didn't worry about how he was going to get to Baker on March 15th. He just reveled in thoughts of Celeste. On February 15th, when the leftover candy went on sale, Tim bought a box and got back to planning Baker's demise. A week later, he still had no idea what he was going to do.

The way he saw it, he had two problems. First, if he wanted to do it on the Ides of March, two-for-one night at Kelly's was out. Second, unless these men were complete fools, they had to at least suspect the other three hadn't been accidents. That meant they'd be careful. They wouldn't be out partying and they certainly wouldn't be getting drunk. He had to change his methods. That didn't mean it wasn't going to happen; it just meant he might not be able to make it look like an accident.

Once again the phone book in the back of the store provided the information he needed. *Fourteen River Street. I know where that is. I used to run past there last fall. Too bad I can't do that now.* If this were 2006, it wouldn't be a problem. Fitness freaks in their spandex running outfits and two hundred dollar running shoes ran all year long then. In 1957, no one ran at this time of year with snow on the ground. If he went out and ran now, he'd stand out like the proverbial sore thumb. He had to think of another way. It came a week later with the winter thaw. One day it was thirty degrees outside, and the next, it was sixty. He still wouldn't be able to run, but a long walk wasn't out of the question.

* * *

Oh, shit. Nothing to see here, just keep on driving, Tim thought when he saw the Barkham police cruiser coming from the other direction. He knew that wasn't going to happen when the red bubble on top lit up. He stopped, stood on the side of the road, and waited for it to stop. As it pulled up, Tim could see the driver was Sheriff Miller.

"You okay?" Miller asked through his open window when he stopped next to Tim.

Tim was puzzled. *Why wouldn't he be okay?* "What?"

"Do you need help? Car trouble, or anything?"

"Oh … no. I'm just out for a walk. I've been cooped up all winter and decided to take advantage of the break in the weather before the cold comes back."

"Okay. Just be careful. And you might want to try walking on the other side so you can see traffic coming."

"Good idea. I never thought of that," Tim answered. He crossed the road as soon as the sheriff drove away because he knew the man would be watching him in his rearview window. He would cross back over as soon as he reached River Street.

River Street was no Ringwood Avenue, but it was a far stretch from the River Street it would become. Fourteen turned out to be an old cape that stood where the upscale River View Condos would go up in 2001. It stood well back from the road and was hidden from its neighbors by pine trees on either side. Tim didn't stop, but he took care to get a good look at the house as he walked by. The most interesting thing about it was that there was a boat and trailer parked on the side of the house. That might have possibilities.

The weather turned cold again two days later, once more confining Tim to his apartment. It was frustrating because the idea that had come to him required warmer weather. If it didn't come, he was going to have to wait for the full moon in May.

The weather broke on Sunday, March 3rd. The temperature only reached fifty degrees, but the promise of warmer weather was in the air. Now, if it just held for another two weeks.

A week before the 15th, Tim realized his plan wasn't going to work. The 15th was a Friday; he worked on

Friday. He would have to get out of work, get to Baker's without being seen, and then get the man to open his door to him. It was a stupid plan, but it was the only one he'd managed to come up with. The May full moon was on Monday, the 13th, his day off. He could definitely make that work. The problem with that was it didn't leave enough time between then and when the carnival returned to deal with both Burke and Miller.

Well, Mister Burke, it looks like you just jumped to the front of the line. I think another visit to your store might be a good idea.

Tim arrived at Burke's T.V. and Appliances just after the store opened at ten o'clock on Monday. Once again, he hadn't been inside more than a few minutes before Burke approached him. "You're back. How's that television working out for you? You ready for a bigger screen yet?"

"Maybe. You have any used ones in the back?"

"Sure I can't interest you in a new one?"

"You got one for twenty dollars?"

"No," Burke laughed. "Let's go in the back and see what I do have."

Tim followed him and thought how easy it would be to just reach out, grab his head, and snap his neck. Easy, but it wasn't going to happen. This was just a reconnaissance mission. Burke lead him past the new televisions and into the appliance section, where there were refrigerators, stoves, and washing machines. "Here you go," Burke told him when they reached the section where the used merchandise was. There were three televisions and two refrigerators. All older models that Burke had taken in trade. "Here we are. How about one of these? They're all twenty-one-inch models. I guess, since you're a repeat customer, I could let you have any of them for twenty dollars."

"I'm tempted, but I live on the third floor over Woolworth's. I'm not sure I could get it upstairs by myself."

"We deliver."

"Free delivery?"

"For new, yes. For one of these ... no."

"Then I guess I'll have to pass, sorry."

Tim turned to leave and still had no idea how he was going to get to Burke. "What if I helped you carry it upstairs myself?" Burke asked just as Tim was about to leave the store.

Tim froze in his tracks. That could work. "You'd do that?"

"Sure. When would be a good time for you?"

"I have Sunday and Monday off. Either of those days would be fine."

"Next Sunday then. The store is closed. Can you be here at noon to help me load it?"

"I can do that."

"Which one do you want?"

"The one with the radio and the turntable."

"Deal. Remember, it's cash only with used sets."

"Right, no problem," Tim assured him.

* * *

Tim arrived at Burke's at noon on Sunday as arranged. The CLOSED sign was hanging on the door, but Burke was waiting and unlocked it when Tim tapped on the glass. "How do you want to do this?" Tim asked when he stepped inside. The T.V. was already there on a dolly.

"I've got a truck outside. We can load it in that, take it over to your building, and then carry it to the third floor."

"That works for me," Tim replied.

Burke propped the door open, and they wheeled the unit to his truck and loaded it into the back.

"Why don't you drive it over and I'll meet you in front of Woolworth's?" Tim told Burke as the man was locking the door to his store.

"You can ride with me if you want," Burke replied.

"It's only a block. I'll have the door open by the time you get there."

When he arrived, Burke was able to park directly in front of Tim's door. "It's a good thing we're doing this today," Tim told him. "On any other day, these spaces are all filled."

Burke looked around at the empty street and had to agree, but now that he was here, he seemed to be in a hurry. "Let's get this unloaded and up to your apartment. This is my only day off, and I've got some things I need to do."

Yeah, me too, Tim thought.

When they got the set off the truck, Tim led the way toward the door. "I'll go up the stairs first. Can you handle the back?"

"Sure, go ahead," Burke answered.

Tim paused once they were inside and at the bottom of the stairs. "Close that door behind you, would you? My landlord has a fit if anyone leaves it open."

Burke nodded, then reached behind him with one arm and pulled the door closed before they started up the stairs.

"It's twenty steps to the top. Let me know if you need to stop."

"I'm fine. Let's just get this done," Burke told him, and Tim could hear the annoyance in his voice.

Tim stopped when he reached the top of the stairs. Burke was still two steps from the top. "What's wrong? Why are you stopping?"

Tim looked Burke directly in the eye before answering. He wanted to see the look on his face when he realized what was happening. "Do you remember going to the Barkham Fair last summer? Do you remember raping that gypsy? "

"What …" Burke started to say and then it hit him. "You're …"

"I'm Death," Tim told him and used one hand to take the tarot card from his shirt pocket. He held it up for Burke to see. Then he shoved.

Burke gave a startled yell before both he and the television went tumbling down the stairs. He hit the bottom in a heap, with the television on top of him. Tim reached him a second later. Burke wasn't dead, but his right arm was bent at an impossible angle. Before he could cry out, Tim grabbed both sides of his head and gave it a violent twist. All the tension went out of Burke's body as his spinal cord snapped.

"What the hell's going on out here?" John Johnson, Tim's neighbor from 2B, called from the top of the stairs.

"We've had an accident here. Do you have a phone?"

"Yes."

"Call someone. The police or an ambulance. Burke's hurt."

Johnson disappeared from the top of the stairs and Tim went outside to wait for whoever was going to arrive. A few minutes later, Johnson joined him at the curb. "I think that man's dead. What happened?"

"We were carrying a television up to my apartment and he slipped on the stairs. Who did you call?"

"The police. They said they'd send an ambulance."

"Good," Tim answered, then heard the wail of a siren.

The ambulance pulled to a stop next to Burke's truck, and Tim watched two attendants get out. "Over there," he told them, pointing to Burke's body in the open door.

The driver walked over and, even though it was obvious Burke was dead, checked the body for a pulse. By the time he walked back to the ambulance to notify the police, a small crowd was gathering. Tim heard murmurs from the onlookers, but the voices of a young boy and his mother stood out above the rest.

"What happened? Is that man dead?"

"Don't look."

"I wanna see."

"No! Let's go. Now!"

The kid tried his best to stay and watch, but his mother managed to drag him away with threats of grounding and no Disneyland on television tonight.

The first police car pulled up five minutes later with its red bubble light flashing and its siren wailing. The cop got out and went directly to the ambulance driver. "What happened here?"

The driver pointed to Tim. "That guy says they were hauling a television set upstairs," then he pointed to Burke, "and that guy slipped and fell. Looks like he broke his neck."

The cop nodded, went over to look at Burke, and then came back to Tim.

"So, what happened?"

Ted related the story he was going to have to tell a dozen times that day. "Mister Burke and I were carrying that T.V. up to my apartment. We got to the top of the stairs and he must have slipped or something. The next thing I knew he was falling down the stairs. I tried to help him, but it was too late. Then my neighbor, John, came to see what had happened. He's the one who called you guys."

It only took a second for the cop to put it together: television … Burke. "Oh shit. That's Bill Burke?"

"Yeah."

"Stay right here. I've got to call the sheriff."

* * *

Cole took the call and slammed the phone down. "God damn it! I told them this was going to happen!" It took him ten minutes to get into his uniform and on the road. He cursed his brother, Burke, and himself the entire time.

When Cole was still a block away, he could see a crowd had gathered in front of Woolworth's. It did nothing to improve his mood. He pulled up to the curb and started barking orders as soon as he was out of his car. "Miles, move these people back. Then get back here and tell me what happened."

"You heard him, people, move back." Most of them only shuffled back a few feet before they stopped. Within a minute, though, they were inching forward again.

"You've got two witnesses over there," he told the sheriff, pointing at Tim and Johnson.

Cole glanced at them and issued another order. "You two, stay right there. I'll get to you in a minute."

Then he went over to look at Burke. "Son of a bitch," he swore before coming back to Tim and Johnson.

"All right, tell me what happened."

Johnson looked at Tim and shrugged as if to say, *You tell him.*

"Mister Burke and I were carrying a television up to my apartment. When we got to the top of the stairs, he must have tripped or something. I heard him grunt, and then he was falling backward down the stairs. The T.V. pulled out of my hands and went down after him. I went down to see if he was hurt, and I found him like that."

When Tim finished, Miller turned to Johnson. "What about you?"

Johnson looked so nervous Tim wasn't sure he was going to be able to tell Miller anything. Once he started talking, though, it all tumbled out in a rush. "I heard this noise out in the hall. It sounded like somebody fell down the stairs. I rushed out to see what had happened and I saw Mister Ritter and Mister Burke at the bottom of the stairs. Mister Ritter told me to call an ambulance or the police, so I went back my apartment and called. Then I came downstairs. I could see Mister Burke was dead, so I came out to wait for the ambulance with Mister Ritter."

"How long was it from the time you heard the noise to when you reached the top of the stairs?"

"I don't know. A minute. Maybe two?"

Miller turned back to Tim. "Why was Burke helping you carry a television? He has help to make deliveries."

"He doesn't offer free delivery on used T.V.s. I couldn't afford to pay to have it delivered. It only cost me twenty bucks. When I told him that, he offered to help bring it over here himself."

Miller had to admit that that sounded like Burke. The man hated to let a buck get away. It sounded like an accident, two witnesses said it was an accident, but Goddammit, it was just too weird to be a coincidence.

* * *

When Tim returned to his room, he burned Burke's tarot card. That only left two — The Moon and The Emperor — Baker and Stu Miller. He knew he would relive Burke's death in his dream tonight and that Celeste would share it. Then they would be back in the woods with Miller ripping her clothes off and throwing her to the ground. Hubie Martin, Bucky St. John, Sawyer Gaunt, and Bill Burke would not be there waiting their turn. Soon Baker would be gone, and only the big man would be left.

Chapter Twenty-One

Stu sat across from Baker trying to calm the man down. "Dammit, Jack, even Cole says this was an accident. There were witnesses. Bill was trying to make a buck and he fucked up. That's all there is to it."

"Yeah, but Cole said this was going to happen. How do you explain that?"

"Coincidence, bad luck, call it anything you want, but it wasn't murder."

"Yeah, well I'm still not convinced."

"Fine. But what are you going to do? Run away and hide?"

"I thought about it."

"And?"

"And I can't afford it. I'd lose my job, and then what?"

"So what are you going to do?"

"I thought I could move in with you for a while. Maybe until Cole figures out what the hell is going on."

"Not only no, but fuck no. Are you out of your mind?"

"No. I just thought I'd ask."

"If you're so fucking scared, why don't get a dog or a gun."

"I hate dogs, and I have a gun. And a dog didn't help Bucky, did it?"

"Bucky got drunk and hit a fucking tree. As fast as he had to be going, anybody in that car would have been killed. Get it through your head. It was a fucking accident. Now get your ass out of here and go home."

As soon as Baker was out the door, Stu reached for the phone. *Fucking Cole. I'm going to kick his ass.*

Cole picked up on the third ring. "What the hell were you thinking telling Baker and Burke that some-body was after them? Baker was just over here all scared and shit and wanting to move in with me."

"Hey, you think what you want, and I'll think what I want, and I'll *tell* who I want. It's no skin off your nose if I'm right or wrong. But it's my ass if I'm right and this shit keeps up. And if I lose my job, you lose your get-out-of-jail-free card. Baker's smart to be wor-ried. And I'll tell you what. If he turns up dead, who-ever's doing this will be coming after you next."

"Yeah, well if you're right, let whoever it is come. If he fucks with me, I'll rip his head off and shit down his throat."

"That's your problem right there, Stu. You think you're the baddest dude in the jungle. The thing is, there's *always* someone badder out there."

Stu was going to answer, but the line went dead.

"Fuck you, too, Cole. And I am the baddest dude around here. If there *is* someone out there, I hope he does come. It'll be the last thing he ever does."

* * *

Idiot, Cole thought when he hung up the phone. *If all of these "accidents" weren't coincidences and someone was picking off Stu's crew, it has to be Tim Ritter. He was there when Burke had his accident. Or maybe Burke was an accident like Ritter says it was and the others weren't. Or maybe they were all accidents. I just don't know. But I still have a bad feeling about it. I'm going to keep an eye on that boy.*

* * *

Cole walked into Woolworth's in uniform at just after eleven o'clock Monday morning. Estella looked surprised when she saw him, then realized why he was there. "Morning, Sheriff. If you're here to see Tim, he has Monday off."

"Actually, I'm here to see Travis. Is he around?"

Estella rolled her eyes. "Of course he's around. He's always around. Where else would he be? He's in the office. You want me to tell him you're here?"

"No, that's okay. I'll go back."

Meek looked up and motioned Miller in when he knocked on the glass of the office door.

"I guess you're here about Bill Burke. That was a terrible thing."

"It was. What can you tell me about your tenant, Tim Ritter?"

"Tim? He works here. He's been here since last summer. He's a good employee, always friendly, always on time. Why?"

"I'm just following up on Burke's accident. He was helping Ritter carry a television up to the third floor. Ritter says Burke tripped and fell down the stairs."

Meek gave the sheriff a hard stare before answering. "What's this about, Sheriff? If it's the stairs, I can assure you, they're in good condition and the lights all work."

It took Cole a second to get what Meek was talking about. "Travis, I'm not worried about that. I know the building's fine. I'm just trying to verify Ritter's story."

"How can I do that? I wasn't there."

"I know that, too, but what can you tell me about Ritter? I don't know the man."

"Tim? Like I said he works for me. He's never been a problem. He's great with the customers and Estella loves the guy. I wish everyone I hired was like him. I'm really going to miss him if he leaves."

"Why would he leave?"

"They all leave. This is a minimum wage job. I gave him a raise after six months, and he'll get another one after a year, but still, it's not enough to raise a family on. One of these days he'll find a girl and that will be that. He'll be looking for something that pays more."

"Where's he from? Not around here."

"New Jersey. He said it was getting too crowded for him down there, so he came to Vermont to find something a little less hectic."

"So, you believe this guy."

"Definitely."

"Okay, Travis. Thanks," Miller said and got up to leave. "I guess that's all I need."

I still don't like it, Cole thought as he left Woolworth's. *It's just too weird. Four of Stu's friends dead in less than nine months. Somebody has to be behind this.*

* * *

Tim knew that someone had to be getting it. Apparently, it was Sheriff Miller. Tim had seen him around town from time to time in the past, but now it seemed like the guy was everywhere. Miller never stopped him, never talked to him, but Tim knew he was watching him. *He wants me to know he's got his eye on me. That's okay; he can't be there all the time. He must suspect that Baker is next, and his brother after that, but he can't prove it. So, like Sherlock Holmes would say, "The game is afoot."*

* * *

When the weather changed and spring finally decided to stay, Tim broke out his sneakers and started running again. He was careful not to let his excursions take him anywhere near River Street. Miller's "Sheriff's Mobile," as he liked to call it, became a common visitor on his outings. The sheriff would approach from one direction, then slow down and stare at Tim before continuing on. A few minutes later he would be back, heading in the opposite direction. Tim never failed to nod and smile at him. He knew he was baiting him, and that it must be driving the man crazy, but he found that he actually enjoyed it. It was a bit of excitement in his otherwise boring routine. He wondered what the sheriff would think if he knew Tim was now carrying Baker's tarot card with him everywhere he went.

Chapter Twenty-Two

Spring brought warm weather, flowers, showers, and the spring thaw. The Connecticut River, which had been frozen most of the winter, was now ice-free and running high and wild. Everything from plastic containers, branches, and even logs were making the journey south toward the Long Island Sound. Tim doubted any of the flotsam would make it that far. It would sink, get snagged along the banks, or get caught up in one of the dams.

Tim felt the tarot card calling to him as May 13th and the full moon approached. He knew what he wanted to do with Baker, he but he still wasn't sure how he was going to be able to get it done. His biggest problem was going to be getting near the man. He had to be spooked. It wasn't until the week before the full moon that inspiration finally struck.

On Saturday night, Sunday morning actually, Tim left the building by the back stairs. He rarely used them because he didn't have a car. When he stepped out into the night, the full moon made it bright enough that he didn't need a flashlight to see where he was going. Once again, he was dressed all in black, making it easy to blend in with the shadows if need be.

Tim only saw one car on his run, jog really, to Baker's. Once there, he was thrilled to see that the Hudson was hooked to the boat and trailer he had seen on his walk. This was better than he had hoped for and it called for a change of plans. He had planned to drown Baker and throw him in the river. This was better. Now all he had to do was wait.

At five, the lights went on in the kitchen. A minute later Tim could see Baker making coffee. *I could sure use a cup of that,* he thought as he sat in the chill morning air.

Baker came out of the house at 5:30 carrying a fishing pole and a tackle box. Tim waited until he was putting the pole in the car before rushing him from behind. Baker heard him coming and wheeled around just in time to face his assailant before Tim rammed into him. The little man was fast, but he stood about as much chance against Tim as Celeste had stood against Stu Miller.

Tim slammed Baker's head into the Hudson hard enough to stun him. The second time he slammed his head into the car, Baker went limp. Tim tied the little man up with a rope he had brought with him, dug his car keys out of his pocket, stuck a rag in his mouth, and tossed him in the Hudson's trunk. The whole thing took less than five minutes.

Within minutes after that, Tim was on the road heading to Butcher's Pond. He hadn't been there since 2001, but he knew how to get there. It had been one of his favorite fishing spots when he had first moved to Vermont in 1970. He was hoping there wouldn't be any other fisherman there at this time of the morning this early in the season.

The last mile of road to the lake was rutted and filled with deep puddles of muddy water. In 2006, the road would still be dirt, but it would be graded and hard packed for easier access to the pond. Tim was glad it was in such sad shape because it discouraged everyone but the most dedicated fisherman from using it. From the lack of tire tracks, he could see that no one had been there in quite some time.

When Tim reached the pond, there was just enough room to turn the Hudson around and back the trailer up to the water. Once it was there, Tim opened the trunk and dragged Baker out. The little man was battered from bouncing around in the trunk on the drive in. He cringed when Tim grabbed him, but his eyes were filled with hatred instead of fear. That would change soon enough.

"You know why you're here, Baker? It's because you're a sadistic little shit who enjoys hurting people. Last summer you and the rest of your asshole buddies raped a young woman at the Barkham Fair. You went last and beat her while you were raping her. I'm here to return the favor. But I'm not going to beat you. I'm going to hold you under the water and look into your eyes while you drown."

Baker tried to struggle when Tim picked him up and slung him over his shoulder in a fireman's carry, but it was useless. When he reached the water, he strode in up to his knees and dropped Baker. The man was trying to scream, but all that came past the rag in his mouth were muffled grunts. "You have any last words?"

Tim asked him, pulling the rag from his mouth.

"I'm sorry! I'm so sorry! Please don't kill me! I'm sorry!"

"Sorry doesn't cut it," Tim told him, then pushed him under and held him there, staring into his eyes until the need for air forced him to breathe. Tim didn't release him until the bubbles stopped coming from his mouth and nose.

Before he left, Tim untied Baker and pushed his body further into the pond. Then he unhooked the boat from the trailer and set it adrift. Satisfied with his work, he took the tarot card from his shirt pocket and burned it. That left only The Emperor.

The hike back to town was a long one, almost eight miles. Tim didn't see the first car until he reached the main road. By then it was eight o'clock and he was jogging like he normally did. People were used to his running by now, so no one would think twice about seeing him.

* * *

Celeste was in Georgia when the heat flooded her body. The troupe was moving north. They would be back in Barkham in two months. She knew when she met Tim in their dream that night that only the big man would be there.

* * *

Baker was missing for over three days before a kid found his car backed up to the lake. The boy didn't think anything of it until his hook snagged on the body. He was using twenty-pound test on the reel. When the line snagged, he carefully reeled it in, trying not to snap it. When Baker's body rose to the surface, the kid dropped the pole, climbed on his bike, and pedaled home as fast as he could. His father was the one who called it in to the Barkham Police Department.

Cole didn't take the call, but he was in his office when it came in to the station. He knew something was wrong when Amy came into the office as soon as she hung up. "A man just called in and said his son snagged a body while he was fishing out at Butcher's Pond."

"Where at Butcher's Pond?"

"At the boat launch. He said there was a car with a boat trailer parked there."

"Oh, shit," Miller swore. "Jack Baker has a boat and trailer." Then to Amy he said, "Call Chambliss and tell him to meet me out at Butcher's Pond."

"You want me to call anyone else?"

"Not until I check it out. It could be nothing more than a dog in the water or something."

Cole drove past Baker's house on his way to Butcher's Pond. He got a sick feeling in his gut when he saw that both the car and boat were missing. *It's Baker, I know it is. How the fuck is this happening?*

Chambliss was already at the boat launch when Miller pulled up. He recognized Baker's Hudson and boat trailer backed up to the shore. "Shit," he swore and parked his car in the middle of the dirt road. Then he walked to the water's edge where Chambliss was standing.

"Anything?" Cole asked when he reached him.

"There's a boat out there," Chris answered, pointing out across the pond.

"You see a body?"

"No, but the kid's pole is right there. I didn't want to touch it until you got here."

"Good thinking," Cole told him, then bent to pick up the fishing pole. Once he had it, he gave it an experimental tug. "There's something on the end of the line. Let's see if I can bring it in without snapping it."

Cole carefully increased the tension on the line until he felt whatever it was on the other end. "It's heavy, whatever it is," he told Chambliss as he slowly took the line up on the reel.

"There! Right there!" Chambliss called out, pointing to a spot about twenty feet off shore.

Cole saw it, too. It was definitely a body. He had it to within ten feet of shore when the line snapped. "Quick, get it before it sinks," he urged Chambliss.

"You get it. I can't swim."

"Damn!" Cole swore and ran into the water to try and grab the body before it was gone. He got to the spot where he had seen it and almost tripped over it. It was resting on the bottom in four feet of water. "Damn," he swore again and knelt down to grab it. The water, which was freezing, came right up to his chin.

Cole dragged the body back to shore by the back of its shirt. "Take him," he told Chambliss when he reached the shore. Once he had passed the body off, he climbed out of the water and stood dripping on the shore. When the adrenalin rush wore off, he realized he was freezing.

"You call for an ambulance. I'm going to get out of these wet clothes," Cole said, and went back to his car for the parka and snow pants he kept in the trunk in case he ever got stuck outside in the winter.

Cole stripped naked, wrung out his wet clothes

as best he could, and put on the snow pants and parka. When he went back to the body, he found Chambliss bending over and puking into the trees on the side of the road. One look at Baker's face told him why. The eyes were gone, eaten by something, snapping turtles probably. The rest of the skin was mottled and had also been fed on. Cole felt his gorge rise, but managed to choke it back.

"Any idea who that is?" Chambliss asked when he managed to rejoin Miller.

"It's Jack Baker. That's his car and trailer."

The fact that Baker was the last of Stu's crew was lost on Chambliss. "Looks like he came out here fishing, had some kind of an accident, and drowned. He wasn't even wearing a life jacket."

Cole was still shivering, even with the dry clothes. "I'm freezing out here. You stay with him. I'm going home to take a hot shower and get into some dry clothes. Call an ambulance and have them take Baker to Wills' Funeral Home. I'll get over there as soon as I can. Tell him not to touch the body until I'm there."

* * *

"What do you want me to do with him, Sheriff?" George Wills asked when Cole arrived at his funeral home.

"I want the medical examiner to look at him. I need to know what happened to him. I'm going to call him and have him do an autopsy."

* * *

Stu was stacking firewood when Cole pulled into

the yard. He looked over at his brother but kept on stacking the wood. "What are you doing up here in the middle of the day?" he asked when Cole came over to where he was working.

"Baker's dead."

That got his brother's attention. "Shit. When did that happen?"

"Sunday morning, I think. He drowned in Butcher's Pond. We just found the body today."

"You said this was going to happen, but I didn't believe you."

"You believe me now?"

"I guess I have to, don't I? You have any idea who it could be?"

"No," Cole lied. "I was hoping you might."

Stu sat back, took a pull on his beer, and shook his head. "No, but I'm going to think about it," he promised.

"If you do think of someone, tell me. Don't go off half-cocked and do something stupid. Remember, I'm the one with the badge."

"Yeah," Stu answered, but Cole knew his brother was already thinking about what he was going to do if he found out who was doing this.

* * *

Cole got the autopsy report three days later. The medical examiner had ruled it an accidental death. He found lake water in the lungs and a head wound consistent with falling and hitting his head on the side of the boat. Cole was so pissed off after reading it that he slammed the report down on his desk. Damn it! It couldn't have been an accident! He was sure of it, but how the hell was he going to prove it? He couldn't.

Chapter Twenty-Three

Tim wasn't surprised when the sheriff seemed to be everywhere in the days following Baker's death. He would slow down and stare at Tim when he found him out on his daily run. Somehow he seemed to know when Tim was eating at Annie's and he would take the seat at the counter directly across from where Tim was sitting. He came into Woolworth's almost daily for something or another, but he never said a word to Tim. He just stared at him for a minute and then left.

Looks like he's figured it out. Maybe I shouldn't have taken Burke out like I did. Well, it's too late to worry about that now. He may suspect what's going on, but he can't prove it or he would have arrested me already. He's just trying to spook me into doing something stupid. He must know Stu's next. Follow me all you want, Sheriff; it's not going to save your brother. And I already know how I'm going to do it.

When it came right down to it, he had always known how he was going to deal with the big man. It was why he had gotten into the shape he was in now. It was why he had honed all the skills he had learned as an army ranger.

On Sunday, June 16th, Tim decided it was time. He'd given the Miller brother's plenty of time to think about what was coming. He'd let a month pass since Baker's death, enough time to allow Stu to relax his guard. No matter how certain the man might be that someone was coming for him, Tim knew it was impossible to maintain a continued state of vigilance for that long. He had learned that in Nam.

Tim had breakfast at Annie's before setting off on the five-mile walk to Stu's place wearing a backpack with a water bottle, three Snickers bars, and a change of clothing. He planned to take his time and arrive at Miller's around two.

* * *

Stu was just starting on his second beer when he heard someone knocking at the door. *Who the fuck could that be*, he wondered as he went to answer it. When he got there, he found a man he didn't know waiting for him. "What," he demanded with a hint of suspicion in his voice.

"It's your turn, asshole. Why don't you come out and we can dance?" the stranger told him.

It took Stu a second to catch on, but when he did, he knew exactly who the man was. "It's you. You're the fucker who killed my crew."

"I am, and now I've come for you. Come out and play."

"I'm going to rip your head off," Stu told the little fucker and stormed out the door.

"Don't you want to know why?" the man asked as he backed away.

"I don't give a fuck why, but go ahead and tell me before *I* kill *you*."

"You remember the woman you raped at the fair last year? She sent me."

"Yeah, well fuck her, too. And I will if she comes back next month."

"I don't think so," the man told him. "Now put your money where your mouth is, you chicken shit."

"This isn't going to take long," Stu told the man, and then rushed him.

* * *

Stu rushed Tim as he knew would: with the over-confidence big men often feel when facing a smaller opponent. The giant was slow, slower than Tim had expected him to be. Maybe it was the beer he had been drinking, or maybe he was used to just wading in and overpowering smaller men. Miller had probably been bullying smaller men since he was a teenager. Tim let him come. Just before he reached him, Tim dodged to the left, lashed out with his left foot, and tripped the big man. Miller sprawled face down in the drive. When he stood up, his face was scraped and bleeding. Tim saw a flash of doubt in the big man's eyes, but it only lasted an instant before it was replaced by anger. When he stood to his full height and sucked in a deep breath, Tim lashed out with his foot and crushed his knee. Miller went down like a broken doll.

"Fucker," the big man spat, and tried to get up. Tim never gave him the chance. He kicked Miller in the face while he was still on his hands and knees. He went down again, this time moaning in pain with a broken jaw.

"Did she moan when you raped her? Did she beg you to stop, or was she stronger than that? I'm betting she was."

Miller rolled onto his back and Tim left him there in the dirt as he walked over to the pile of firewood stacked on the side of the house. He picked a heavy piece of oak from the pile.

By the time he got back, Miller had regained his feet. Tim had to admit he had balls, but balls weren't going to help him. "She wanted you to suffer like you made her suffer," Tim told him. Then he drove his right foot into Miller's other knee. The big man went to his knees with a gasp of pain. Miller didn't scream until Tim brought the piece of oak down on his left arm. He repeated the process on the other arm. Then he stepped back and spit on him. By this time, Miller was sobbing and begging for mercy.

"Not going to happen, big man. Today's the day you join the rest of those assholes in hell." Tim dropped the oak and crushed Miller's trachea with a wicked karate chop. Then he stood and watched the fear in the big man's eyes turn to panic when he realized he couldn't breathe. Tim didn't turn away until the life drained out of him. Now he only had one more asshole to deal with.

Cole.

The man hadn't raped Celeste, but he had protected the men who had. That was the only way to close the circle.

When Tim got back to his room, he burned The Emperor card.

When Celeste felt the burn, she knew that Tim had

dealt with the last of her rapists. The cloud that had hovered over her for almost a year was gone. Tonight they would share the dream she had been waiting for. The big man was finally gone. Tim had done it. When she woke, she knew she would never have that particular dream again and that in three weeks she would be in Barkham with the man who was her destiny.

* * *

Cole found his brother when he came to check on him that night. This time there was no way it could be mistaken as an accident. Stu was lying on his back in the dirt, staring at the sky. He had been beaten to death.

That fucking Ritter. I'm going to kill that son of a bitch myself. He wanted to go after the man right now, but he couldn't just leave Stu lying in the dirt. Not his brother.

Cole went into the house, pulled the sheet off Stu's bed, and went outside to cover the body. Once that was done, he went back in the house and called the station on Stu's phone. He didn't want any dipshits listening in on a scanner to hear it and spread it all over town. If that happened, the place would be swarming with assholes

Cole was about to hang up and use his radio when Terry Chambliss finally picked up. "Sheriff's office."

"Terry, it's Cole. I need you to get yourself out to my brother's place. No lights and no sirens. I want this kept quiet, you understand?"

"Sure, Cole. What's going on? Is Stu all right?"

"I'll tell you when you get here. Now move your ass."

Cole secured the scene and took pictures of his brother's body while he waited for Chambliss. He gathered evidence and took notes. He considered calling in the state police, but he didn't want their interference. He knew who did this and he was going to take care of it himself. Being sheriff in a hick Vermont town had its perks.

Chapter Twenty-Four

Tim was eating breakfast at Annie's when Cole came in and sat at the counter opposite him. If looks could kill, as the old saying goes, Tim's heart would have stopped on the spot. Instead of glancing away, Tim stared back. "Have a seat, Sheriff. We should talk," he said before their war of wills became apparent.

The invitation obviously took Cole by surprise, but he recovered quickly. "Yeah, maybe we should," he agreed, and joined Tim in the booth.

It was ten o'clock on a Monday morning, half way between the morning rush and lunch, so they practically had the place to themselves.

"I'll talk, you listen," Tim told him, confident no one could overhear them.

"This was all your fault, you know. You and your brother's."

"What do you mean my fault?"

"A young woman came to you last summer and

told you that your brother and his friends had raped her. You blew her off. You asked her what she did to encourage them. Then you asked her how much she charged. You knew your brother and the rest of them raped her, and you protected them. You sanctioned it. In my eyes, that makes you as guilty as them. How many other times did that happen? How many other women did they rape? How many lives did you let them ruin?"

Miller sat back and Tim could see the anger drain from the man as what he had just been told sank in.

"So where do we go from here, Sheriff? You know what happened, but you can't prove it. There's no way you can connect me to any of those accidents. If you arrest me, your part in all this will come out. I don't think you have it in you to kill me. It takes a mindset you don't have. I didn't have it until the army taught me how to be a killer."

When Miller didn't answer, Tim went on. "I'll be leaving soon. I'd advise you to just let this go. If you can't … well … if you can't, then whatever happens … happens."

Then Tim slid a card, face down, across the table toward Miller. The sheriff turned it over and laid it face up between them. "What's this?"

"It's a tarot card. The Fool. It means you're about to start on a new life. Where you take it is up to you."

Then he got up, dropped a five on the table, and walked out.

* * *

"Oh, I've got it, and I'm going to do to you what you did to the others," Cole said to Ritter's back as the man walked out of Annie's. "But first I have to bury my brother."

Stu's wake was held the following Friday at Wills' Funeral Home. Cole hadn't expected many people to come since his crew had preceded him, but when no one at all came, he realized just how much his brother had alienated the entire town. The burial on Saturday was more of the same. Cole was the only mourner there.

He was devastated. He had suspected something like this, but had never dreamed it was his fault. If he had listened to the gypsy and arrested Stu and the rest of them, they'd all be alive today. Maybe that's what Stu and the rest had needed all along. It might have made a difference to some of them.

Worse, he knew Ritter was right. He didn't have it in him to kill him. He was going to have to live with the consequences of his actions. He wasn't sure he could.

* * *

On Tuesday morning, Tim gave Meek his two-week notice and told him he'd be moving out of the apartment. "I'm sorry to hear that. You've been a good employee and tenant. Where are you going?"

"I'm not sure. It's just time for a change. Maybe I'll try Maine or New Hampshire." Tim had no intention of telling anyone that he'd be joining the carnival when it returned.

Estella was more upset about Tim's leaving than Meek seemed to be. "I knew this was going to happen. I really like you, Tim. You remind me of my son." He almost laughed when she told him that. *Oh, Stell. If you only knew. If you did, I might remind you of your father.*

Tim kept up his routine while he waited for Celeste and the carnival to return. He worked, he ran, and he stopped in at Annie's twice a week for breakfast and dinner. He only saw the sheriff twice, and each time the man avoided his eyes.

The day before the carnival was to arrive in Barkham, Tim looked around the apartment to decide what to take with him. In the end, all he opted for was his clothes. He'd leave the rest for the next tenant. He really didn't need anything else, and there wouldn't be room for it in Celeste's trailer anyway.

In the morning, he showered and dressed in the clothes he had laid out the night before, stuffed his toiletries in the backpack, dropped his keys off at Meek's office, and went to Annie's for one last breakfast.

"Tim, did you hear about Sheriff Miller?" Tina asked as soon as he was through the door. "Ted Swanson found him in his cruiser this morning. He killed himself. He was a friend of yours, wasn't he?"

"Not really. I only knew him to talk to him. What happened?"

"Nobody really knows. I guess his brother's murder really got to him. I hear they still don't have any idea who did it."

"That's too bad. I hope they catch whoever it is."

"So what are you having? The usual?" Tina asked as she set a cup of coffee in front of him.

"The usual sounds good."

When he left Annie's, he shouldered his backpack and started on the walk that would take him to his new life. The only things he knew for sure about it were that he would spend it with Celeste and that he would be in Wayne, New Jersey on September 3rd, 1964. He had one last rapist to deal with. No, make that one would-be rapist to deal with.

Epilogue

Barkham, Vermont, July, 2006

Tim stared at the key that he hadn't used in fifty years. It was strange to think that, by the calendar, just yesterday he had used it to lock the door he now stood in front of. He had given up trying to reconcile the vagaries of having lived two separate lives between 1956 and 2006. For those fifty years, there had been two of him, or at least he thought there had been. He had never gone in search of his other self to confirm it. Now that the day he had "gone back" had passed, he was back to being the one and only Tim Ritter. And now that the other him was gone, there were loose ends that needed to be tied up, a life to live that had been put on hold for fifty years.

Celeste followed him into his past. She was fascinated by the pictures on the walls and mantle. They depicted a life Tim had lived before they had met. She stood in front of the one of Tim in Vietnam for a long time. "What was it like over there?" she asked.

"Hard, but without that time, I never would have been able to do what I did when you brought me back," he answered.

Tim let her explore the house while he retrieved the spare set of car keys from the pegboard in the kitchen. Eventually, they would need to decide what to do with the house — sell it, keep it as a summer home, or give it to Tim Junior and his wife. He had considered never coming back to it, but that would have caused too many problems. In 2006, you couldn't just disappear: there were too many electronic ropes tied to you to do that — taxes, social security checks, doctors who knew you were dying of cancer. No, he would pick up the threads of this life and see where they took them.

"Ready to go?" he asked Celeste after she had been through the entire house.

"Yes, but I want to come back after we get your car."

"No problem," he answered.

"You want to go in?" he asked her when they got to the fair grounds. He could tell she was tempted, but she declined.

"No," she finally answered. They had walked away from that life in 1964 and Celeste had no desire to go back.

"Fine, I'll meet you back at the house," he told her. Then he got out and walked toward the parking lot. It was the last day of the fair, the day after he had gone back. It took him almost an hour to find the car. He remembered a lot of things from back then, but where he had parked the car was not one of them.

ABOUT THE AUTHOR

Dan Foley is the author of the novels *Reunion*, *Death's Companion, Abandoned and Wolf's Tale*, *The Whispers of Crows*, a collection of short stories, and the novella, *Intruder*. Dan is a New Jersey native who now lives in Connecticut. Before retiring and embarking on his new career as an author, Dan was a licensed Senior Reactor Operator. He taught reactor power plant operations at several nuclear power plants in the U.S. as well as China.

Also by Dan Foley

Something lurks beneath the surface of Cooper Lake.
Something hungry. Something intelligent.
Something that preys on those who venture too close to its
domain.
The native Indians had a name for it.

ONIARE

In 1939, its victim was a young drifter. Dave Longo fought and
killed it then, but it won't stay dead.
It returned in 1956 to claim the lives of two young men. For
Dave, its return was a reunion in Hell.
It's now 2014 and the creature has returned again, but Dave
Longo is not around to face it a third time. The task becomes
the responsibility of Ryan Lowell, a child the oniare had
terrorized back in '56, but can he overcome his childhood fears
to vanquish the oniare once and for all.

And check out these other titles from
Grinning Skull Press

"I killed my parents when I was thirteen years old."
And now, with the murder of Missy Blake twenty-two
years later, it's time for Jack Greene to finish what he
started.

When the co-ed's mutilated body is found, the police
are clueless, but Jack knows what killed the pretty
college student; he's been hunting it for years. The
hunt has been going on for too long, though, and Jack
wants to end it, but he can't do it alone. The local
police aren't equipped to handle the monster in their
midst, so Jack recruits Major Kelly Langston, and
together they set out to rid the world of this
murdering creature once and for all.

"A suspenseful, twisty ride! Heart-pounding horror!"
–L.X. Cain, author of *Bloodwalker* and *Soul Cutter*

WELCOME TO THE DANDY DROP INN,
WHERE EVERYBODY
IS TREATED LIKE FAMILY!

It's the worst snowstorm Missouri has ever seen, and nine strangers, each harboring their own secrets, find themselves sharing a roof at the Dandy Drop Inn.

CHECKING IN'S EASY, …

Jim and Dolores Dandy wouldn't dream of turning anybody away, especially not on the worst night in Missouri's history, because that just wouldn't be neighborly.

… CHECKING OUT'S A BITCH.

Before the storm is over, blood will flow.

Who will survive to see the storm finally pass?

SUBSTRATUM

A Jasper O'Malley Novel

Deep beneath the streets of Detroit, someone — or something — is picking off the miners of the Detroit Salt Combine. The company knows what it is. They thought they could control it.

They were wrong.

Now it's running free and it has a taste for human flesh.

Only one man can stop it: Jasper O'Malley, an Attican Detective Agent with a reputation for getting the job done. But once Jasper sees the creature, he has his doubts. This time, has he bitten off more than he can chew?